The Third Door

Mark Eugene Langner

Aliso Street Productions

To Wayne, my Woodsward

* * * *
*

This is a work of fiction. Any similarity between characters and real persons, living or dead, is purely coincidental.

THE THIRD DOOR
TABLE OF CONTENTS

PART ONE

One	Tumbling	1
Two	Eator	18
Three	Yutor	29
Four	Beyond the Wooden Wall	42
Five	Madness	62
Six	The stones are thrown	74
Seven	Choosings	86

PART TWO

Eight	The Third Door	93
Nine	Breaking of arms	112
Ten	Many partings	124
Eleven	Many dreams	143

PART THREE

Twelve	Kaden's mission	158
Thirteen	Tordawn	171
Fourteen	Forsaken places	186
Fifteen	Meeting the Master	200
Sixteen	Yodin	211
Seventeen	Wrack and ruin	220
Eighteen	Party plans	228
Nineteen	The Diversionary	238

PART FOUR

Twenty	Lessons	248
Twenty-one	Child's play	261
Twenty-two	Extempore	272
Twenty-three	Arcane exit	284
Twenty-four	Perpetuity	295

The Third Door

PART ONE

CHAPTER ONE
Tumbling

The moon looked out of place in the afternoon sky, as if it had been dropped and forgotten. Nobody noticed it now, Thayn thought to himself. He glanced around at the busy marketplace and wondered what – if anything – it meant.

He needed to concentrate. How? Banners atop high stone walls fluttered in the breeze. Below them colorfully dressed customers walked this way and that, some with intention, others laughing among themselves as vendors called to them. A variety of smells, earthy, sweet and savory, mingled in the air.

The marketplace was shaped like a wedge, one of six public areas that surrounded the core of the city. Behind Thayn were wooden tables of vegetables and grains. The walls on either side were lined with household wares to the far end of the marketplace where booths sold refreshments.

The core of Eator was the ancient stone Center. Cylindrical and monolithic, it towered over the city. Leafy trees under its curved wall offered shade to tables where people paused to eat and relax. Thayn wished that he were with them.

He stood on the edge of the exposition area. It was usually an open space stacked with coarsely woven, brightly colored bristlecloth, but not this afternoon – spectators presently surrounded it.

"Excuse us. Pardon us. Coming through." A robust woman in an orange homespun gown pushed her way through the crowd. She was Zylla, Thayn's stepmother. His father, Zayn, followed in her wake, and his mother, Kalia, trailed behind them. They also wore orange. Other spectators wore red, purple, yellow and blue, all of the same brittle weave. "Up ahead. Coming through."

Zylla squeezed them into a spot along the exposition area. There were complaints behind them until she turned and frowned. The grumbling stopped.

Thayn spotted his mother and waved. Kalia waved back. He took a deep breath and gave a little shrug. Together, their green eyes danced.

Thayn looked at his father. He often imagined that

his father talked to him. An undeniable voice in his head offered Thayn guidance and companionship. Zayn seemed to smile, looking in no particular direction.

Hair fell across his face. Zylla brushed Zayn's brow and Thayn brushed his own. They looked alike, father and son.

"Don't worry, son," Thayn heard his father say. "You'll do well. You're strong and talented. You'll be rewarded."

Zylla called and waved. "Here we are." Her voice warbled and she showed a lot of teeth.

This afternoon the marketplace, in addition to its daily business, hosted a tumbling contest. The representative from Nexus Four was on the floor, tall and wiry with kinky brown hair. His blue uniform was of a prize weave, thin and stretchy. There was a burst of applause, especially from others dressed in blue, as he finished his routine with a circle of cartwheels.

Thayn, in orange, stood with his stepsister, Ava, and his best friend, Rykos. They wore orange, too.

"You're better than that," Rykos concluded as Thayn pulled gingerly at the sleeves of his own uniform. He represented his community, Nexus Six. Rykos looked at him encouragingly. "If you win, I'll buy

3

you a leafcake from Boz' booth."

Ava pouted her lips. "You just want to go there anyway," she objected. She had loosened her long red braid and recoiled it deftly on top of her head, securing it into place with a wooden pin.

"Ouch," Rykos mimicked her.

"Oh, be quiet. Besides, aren't you going to stay and watch me?" Ava would join the drummers.

"Do what? Boom, boom, boom."

"Thayn?" she appealed.

Thayn wasn't listening. The next competitor took the floor. His name was Arlos and he was from Nexus Five. Thayn watched him. He was broad across, but slim, and almost disappeared when he turned sideways. His hair hung in tangles, uneven shades of brown.

Thayn usually looked away when he saw Arlos. Arlos made Thayn feel self-conscious. Now everyone watched him. Nobody would notice if Thayn did, too.

Arlos wore yellow. He stood as if he were in a dream that Thayn might have of him. When Thayn looked at Arlos an awkward feeling came over him. He could hear his heart pounding in his ears. He worried, could everyone hear it?

For this reason Thayn avoided Arlos everywhere they went – but never in his thoughts. Not for several years – he remembered the moment that it happened. The morning after his father's so-called accident, on their way to school, Arlos looked – *different* – to him.

And now he stood not ten feet in front of him, so – *real*. Arlos stretched in preparation for his performance. He was more substantial than Thayn imagined, the thin, stretchy weave of his yellow uniform accentuating everything that it attempted to conceal. As Thayn watched Arlos he sensed the world run on without him. Something was unveiled to him, but Thayn cared only that Arlos stood in front of him, and it was warm and bright, and the weight of the world had lifted and the crowd was cheering –

"Not to worry," Rykos interrupted.

"What?"

"He's no competition. You're better than that," Rykos gestured at Arlos.

"What?" Thayn repeated.

"What a dut."

Who – Arlos? "Dut" was a word that Thayn and Rykos had made up. It wasn't complimentary.

"Dut?" Thayn asked angrily. For some reason he wanted to hit Rykos. Rykos took a step back.

Two teachers in green gowns stood nearby. Yara, the younger of them, watched Arlos prepare for his routine, her plain features unorganized into any particular expression. Elyda, however, watched Thayn. She was an old woman with a face full of wrinkles. After she caught his eye, Thayn checked his behavior and looked away.

"What's wrong with you?" Rykos asked in earnest. "Are you – ?"

"Hush," Ava scolded them both.

Arlos had begun. He ran forward and tumbled several times, then stretched upright, standing on his hands. He held absolutely still and the crowd cheered.

Thayn and – warily – Rykos returned their attention to him.

Arlos sprang backward and landed on his feet. He stood still again, first with his arms outstretched. Then he brought them to his side. Arlos' shoulders were straighter than his own, Thayn thought, and broader.

He ran forward again, tumbling through the air. He found his feet only to leap again. The crowd responded enthusiastically, especially those dressed in yellow. Another set of cartwheels brought him closer to Thayn. Arlos' features were thin and his expression was narrow with concentration. Cool gray eyes looked through Thayn. Arlos leapt sideways, finishing with a succession of wheels and dives.

He flew through the air like leaves in the wind – but he was clearly a man. Thayn wanted to be like him – no, it was more than that. Thayn wanted to *be* him – no – to *have* –

Thayn didn't know what he wanted.

For a moment everything stood still. Watching Arlos made Thayn feel incapable of living in the world without him. Thayn realized that, apart from Arlos, he would be empty inside.

Arlos finished his routine. It took some time for the applause to subside. Thayn stared unabashedly as Arlos bowed to the crowd and held one arm high.

"Thayn," Ava whispered. "It's your turn."

"What?" Thayn felt immediately incapable of his task. Why had he agreed to do this?

He quickly took his place and stretched a little. He tugged at his uniform and smoothed it. Everyone was watching. Thayn waited for his father's voice in his head, words of encouragement that he imagined his father would say to him.

"My boy – my *man*. How strong you have become, and how handsome. You must do well so I may reward you." But it wasn't his father's voice that he heard this time. It was Arlos'.

Thayn had practiced his routine often and knew it

by heart. A good thing, because he didn't remember this performance, neither during nor after it. It was an ambitious sequence of tumbles and flips and stands. All Thayn remembered was a blur as he spun through the air. Purples and reds, other colors of the crowd, cheering, the blue of the sky and bright yellow sunlight, and shadow, cool and gray – Arlos' eyes.

Thayn blinked and shook his head. His routine was over. Applause continued. And still, there in front of him – those eyes – it was Arlos, congratulating him. "Very nice." Arlos clasped Thayn by the shoulder. They smiled together, their lips merely inches apart. Thayn could hear his heart pounding. That feeling of awkwardness redoubled.

Arlos turned to leave. No. He must not falter. Thayn had to tell him. How else would Arlos know? "I want – "

Arlos turned back again. "Yes – ?"

They were interrupted by a cry from the crowd. The winner of the match was announced, and he was neither Thayn nor Arlos. Instead the first competitor, a young man from Nexus Two, won. Everyone in the crowd clapped appreciatively, especially those dressed in purple who whistled and cheered for their champion.

Several schoolmates in yellow congratulated Arlos,

adding, "Your parents are waiting for you."

Arlos shrugged good-naturedly. "Tomorrow," he offered, "we'll talk at school."

"In the garden." Thayn closed his eyes. He whispered, already imagining their meeting. "Yes."

He opened his eyes dreamily. Arlos was gone. Rykos stood in his place, accompanied by Ava. "Yes what?" Rykos asked. He handed Thayn an orange tunic.

Thayn grabbed it and pulled it on over his uniform. "Nothing."

"Anybody mention you're getting a little touchy lately?" Rykos didn't wait for an answer, continuing, "Too bad you didn't win. I'll buy you a leafcake anyway."

"See," Ava objected, "what did I tell you? What about me?"

Elyda and Thayn's parents joined them. Thayn prepared himself to be hugged by Zylla. She oversqueezed him. "Our boy," she said more to Elyda than anyone else.

Released from her embrace, Thayn hugged his father, who didn't respond. He looked at his mother. As always, he found comfort in her eyes. She extended a hand and he held it in both of his.

"Thayn, come on. Boz' booth, remember?"

"Do you want to visit the bakers?" Elyda asked in a patronizing tone.

"Yes," Rykos replied.

Ava contradicted him. "He wants to visit Aryla." She was Boz the baker's daughter.

Elyda smiled. "I see." Elyda was a Ministrant. She and the other women of the Ministration attended to the needs of the city, especially the affairs of the Genexus. Her role as teacher was one of many. She also sat on the High Council. The welfare of the city was her calling and through the Genexus she lived her life. She knew more about them than they knew about themselves.

The other teacher joined them. She was Yara, a young Ministrant who taught the early grades. "Hello, Rykos. And Thayn, well done. And Ava."

Ava's expression changed.

"How nice you look. Will you be drumming for the dancers?" Yara asked her. "Or could we talk?"

Ava was seldom at a loss for words. "Thank you – yes – no – if you – I – " she stammered, melting and beaming. Rykos and Thayn rolled their eyes. Wasn't she suddenly teacher's pet?

Just then Arlos and his parents came into view.

They browsed the nearby weavers' tables. Thayn's heart skipped a beat.

*

With a knowing smile Elyda watched it all, blinking. She thought to herself, "These children are beyond their time. Jovia must throw their stones and determine their Choosings. I must tell her."

*

"Come on," Rykos whispered. Then he said aloud to Thayn's parents, trying his best to exclude Elyda whom he didn't trust, "I promised Thayn a leafcake if he did good."

"'He did well,'" Elyda corrected him.

"Yes, he did," Zylla agreed wholeheartedly.

"May we?" Thayn asked.

"Well – " Zylla sucked her teeth.

"Yes, of course," Kalia replied, smiling.

"We'll be back in time to hear Ava drum." Ava didn't seem to hear them. She directed all her attention to Yara.

Rykos began in the direction of Arlos and his parents. Thayn hadn't the nerve. "Let's go this way," he called, pointing in the opposite direction.

"It's longer," Rykos complained, but Thayn already slipped away and Rykos hurried to catch up with him. Before he had a chance to explain, Thayn ran into the wiry competitor from Nexus Four. With him were two of his classmates in bright blue gowns.

"Thayn."

"Edos."

"You know Miara and Weela." Miara was delicate and very pale. Blonde hair fell in a plait down her back. Weela, short and stout, wore her hair closely cropped.

Every nexus of the city had separate classrooms in the school. Thayn recognized Miara and Weela but didn't know them well. "Yes," he responded politely.

"Miara wants you to know – " Edos' voice had a mocking edge to it.

Weela giggled. She knew that Edos was jealous of Thayn because Miara had smiled at him during his routine.

"Don't, Edos," Miara interrupted, flushing.

" – she liked your performance."

"Edos, no," she pleaded.

"She's shy," he concluded. His remarks were intended for Miara, not Thayn. There was an uncomfortable pause. They all looked at one another. Weela giggled some more.

"All right, then," Thayn replied softly. With a nod

he turned to leave. He felt a hand on his shoulder and turned back.

"I don't believe we've finished our visit," Edos said, glancing at Miara. He spoke more loudly. "She *liked* it, if you know what I mean."

Thayn wasn't sure that he did. More than embarrassed now, Miara seemed upset. Was Edos angry? At whom? Her or Thayn? "Don't, Edos," she pleaded.

Rykos caught up with them. So did Edos' parents.

"What's going on here?" Edos' father demanded. He, too, was tall and wiry. Edos' mother had kinky brown hair.

"He's been discourteous to Miara," Edos alleged.

Rykos objected, "No way."

"Edos," Miara objected, too. She turned from pink to crimson.

Weela, despite her best efforts, continued to giggle.

"Perhaps you should apologize, young man."

"I didn't do anything – I barely know her," Thayn tried to explain.

Arlos and his parents joined them. His parents looked like Arlos, broad at the shoulder, but slim, with gray eyes that looked right through Thayn.

"I – " Thayn stopped short. His heart was already pounding. "I intended no disrespect."

Arlos looked from Thayn to Miara and back again. "Oh." *Every*thing was awkward now.

"No – I – " Thayn tried to explain. "Arlos – it's not – not – what you – "

"I see." Edos looked from Thayn to Arlos and back again. He repeated himself with greater exaggeration. "I *see*."

Edos' father frowned. "See what, son?"

"Miara, you're picking your fruit from the wrong tree, I think."

After a moment Edos' mother asked, "What does that mean, dear?"

Thayn flushed.

Miara burst into tears. Edos' mother went to comfort her.

"You'd better shut up." Rykos was pushing on Edos' chest.

Arlos' mother stepped between them. Her gray eyes grew severe.

Thayn shook his head. "Rykos, no."

Arlos stood in front of his mother. "Thayn?"

"I'm going to call a Monitor," Edos' father decided.

"No, please, don't. I –" Thayn's parents came into view. Miara looked out from Edos' mother's arms.

"All right. I apologize, Mira – Mari – " He couldn't
say her name right.

Miara cried louder and buried her head.

"I'm sorry," Thayn repeated to everyone. Then he
pulled Rykos away. "Come on."

"Go," Edos' father agreed.

"Next time – " Edos took a step after him.

"Edos," his mother scolded him, "he said he was
sorry."

*

Thayn and Rykos escaped the exposition area and
hurried past hardware booths to the back of the marketplace. At a table under the leafy trees they sat and
caught their breath. "What happened to you?" Rykos
asked.

"Me? What happened to *you*?" Hair fell across his
brow and, by habit, Thayn brushed it away. "You almost got in a fight."

"Over you. He insulted you."

"What?"

"He said you – that Arlos – that – he suggested – "
Several whiskers grew from Rykos' chin. He pulled
on them, thinking for a moment, looking at Thayn curiously until he flushed. "But you got mad at me, too,
when I – "

Thayn flushed even more.

"Then it's true?"

Thayn didn't answer.

"Is it?"

Thayn turned away from him.

"It doesn't matter, Thayn," Rykos added hastily. "It's perfectly all right if you – if it – is. I just didn't know, that's all. It's not like with Ava – so obvious."

Thayn turned back. "What? With Ava?"

"Yes."

"Obvious?"

"With *Ya*-ra." Rykos said her name with a lilt.

"What?"

"You don't see it?"

"No."

"Oh, please. She absolutely falls apart every time *Ya*-ra comes near her. The same way – the way you do with – "

Thayn looked away again.

" – with – what's his name?"

"Arlos."

"With *Ar*-los," Rykos repeated. Did he say his name funny, too?

"How do *you* know?" Thayn asked, suddenly angry. He glared at him. "Since when did you become

16

the expert on – ?"

"*Ry*-kos?" came a coo from behind him. Thayn watched Rykos' ears turn bright red. They sat not far from the bakers' booths. Aryla joined them. Short and doughy, a confection in pink, she was obviously, for Rykos, the sweetest thing behind the counter. Why hadn't Thayn figured it out sooner?

"A-*ry*-la," Rykos greeted her.

They stood. "Hello, Thayn."

"Aryla," Thayn returned, smiling.

Aryla smiled at Rykos. "I have to run a quick errand. Father needs more redfruit. I'll be right back. We saved you a leafcake. Father has it. Oh, and *Ry*-kos?"

"Yes?"

"You'll still walk me home, won't you?"

"Of course."

After Aryla left, Thayn said, "I see. You *are* an expert."

CHAPTER TWO
Eator

Boz, the baker, was a favorite personality. With a wink and a quick grin he made everyone feel special. His booth was one of the most popular places in the marketplace.

"Finally you're here," Boz welcomed Thayn and Rykos. Himself as short and doughy as his daughter, Boz' face was florid in the afternoon heat. There was a line waiting, especially now that Aryla had run her errand. "Congratulations, Thayn. You performed well."

How could he know, Thayn wondered, when Boz was here working?

"Come close. We saved the last leafcake for you," Boz whispered. Then he told them much too loudly that they were responsible for the salt in his salt-and-pepper hair. Boz told every youngster of the city the same thing, pointing every time to a different twist of gray. Always he laughed, and his laughter was always the same.

"Would you like me to help you with the counter?" Rykos asked.

"There's a good boy," Boz replied, "but it would be less trouble if you didn't. Your cake's in back. Eat it there if you like."

Boz' establishment was next to last in the row of food booths. Thayn and Rykos hurried between Boz and his neighbor's booths to a narrow service area that ran along the high wall of the Center. The back room was dim compared to the sunshine outside and Boz' customers couldn't see them devour their leafcake.

Ava and Yara came to the booth. "Look. What did I tell you?" Rykos whispered. In Ava's company, Yara looked almost pretty. Ava looked uncharacteristically self-conscious.

Thayn cocked his head and repeated what he overheard Yara say. "She's going to find them a table."

Ava evidently had forgotten about drumming for the dancers or no longer cared about it. "May I have two honey dumplings, please?" she asked Boz.

Kinky hair appeared behind her. Edos and his parents waited next in line. Thayn gestured for Rykos to move closer and they watched.

"Ahem."

"Yes?" they heard Ava ask.

"I'm Edos. You're Ava."

"Yes."

"I've been *aware* of you." He smiled – clearly confident that she knew what he meant – and looked at her with intention.

Edos' mother coughed a little.

"Oh, yes, and these are my parents."

"Hello." Ava took her honey dumplings, thanked Boz, and, without another word, slipped away.

"Well," sniffed Edos' mother.

"She doesn't seem like a very nice girl," decided his father.

"Father," Edos protested.

"Not as nice as Miara. Or Weela."

"Mother, please." He flushed.

Thayn and Rykos didn't dare look at each other until Edos and his parents left. Then they both burst out laughing. "Do they know so little?" Thayn asked.

"Parents? Or maybe they've forgotten." They returned their attention to their leafcake. It was their favorite, soft and crunchy.

When Thayn looked up again, Arlos stood at the counter. "Oh," he exclaimed.

"What?" Rykos looked up, too.

Aryla had returned with redfruit and joined her father from the front of the booth. She waited on Arlos. Thayn and Rykos, squinting against the sunlight, watched them.

The table nearest the booth became available and Arlos and his parents sat at it. Thayn looked out at them through the doorway. They ate mellowpuffs. Arlos bit into one slowly and licked at its filling.

A breathless young woman hurried through the back of the booth. "Hello, Rykos."

"Hello, Ingra."

She tied on an apron and brushed against Thayn as she passed, returning him to the moment. "Sorry I'm late." She and Aryla traded places.

"I'm ready," Aryla announced, joining Rykos.

Thayn followed them out the back of the booth. Rykos took Aryla by the arm. She stopped him and they turned around. "*Ry*-kos, where are your manners? Say goodbye to Thayn."

"Oh, right, sorry." Rykos' ears turned red again. "Goodbye, Thayn. See you tomorrow."

"Right." He smiled at Rykos. "Goodbye, Aryla."

Their path would take them past Arlos and his parents, anyway. Ava and Yara still sat at a nearby table. Thayn gladly walked the other way through the service area to the far path.

Vendors advertised their wares. More booths offered items for the house and garden, pots and pans and shovels and hoes. Thayn hurried past them to reach the exposition area. How different it looked now. Young men and women danced without reserve as friends beat drums of various sizes and shapes. *Boom boom tap a tap boom tap a tap.* The produce booths were nearly empty of their daily yield.

Thayn slipped through one of several arches that opened in the massive stone wall surrounding the marketplace and entered the busy Great Path. Everyone in Eator seemed to have somewhere to go at the moment. Colorfully dressed Genexus passed in either direction.

The Great Path surrounded a swath of public buildings that hugged the Center of the city. After the marketplace came the smithies, the library, the school, the auditorium, the temple and then the marketplace again.

Between every public building was an inner path to the Center. Beyond the Great Path, as walled outer paths, they defined six nexus. Within them resided the greater population of the city.

Thayn dodged his way across the Great Path and disappeared under the arch of Nexus Six.

*

The dwellings of Nexus Six rose immediately, tall and squished together. Walkways among them were narrow and crooked. Thayn lived down a path to the right. He was in no hurry and turned the other way.

Unlike the public buildings that had been planned with precision, the stone dwellings of the Genexus had been dismantled and rebuilt informally, enlarged and reduced, connected and separated and altered countless times. Even now, up ahead, new rooms were being built and Thayn had to renegotiate his course. He and his neighbors waved to one another. Some had seen the contest. "You should have won," they called.

"Thanks," Thayn called back.

As he entered the fields the dwellings became free-standing and farther apart. Snug under shady trees, some had little gardens all their own. Rykos and his parents lived along one of several rutted lanes.

The fields were fertile and carefully tended. Thayn followed a path bordered on one side by grains, fruit and vegetables and on the other side by bristle for weaving and herbs for dyes.

Thayn didn't understand why most people seemed to prefer the cramped quarters that he and his family shared closer to the Great Path. He liked it better out here. His shoulders lowered and his stride eased. The air smelled sweet. He looked out into the far fields. They reached to the Wooden Wall, a vast defense around Eator.

Thayn wondered if Rykos was home yet. No, what was he thinking? Rykos was with A-*ry*-la.

He passed a derelict structure. Thayn knew who lived there. Axl.

*

Thayn had only seen Axl from a distance, except once when he was very young. He barely remembered Kalia screaming at Axl, "Leave us alone." He was a crazy man, she warned her son.

Axl ran outside whenever it stormed. On his way to visit Rykos, Thayn often saw Axl dancing in the far fields. "He'll be struck by lightning," everyone always said, but he never was.

*

The path looped back in the direction of the city. Thayn passed the last few trees and imagined, under them, a little home of his own – there was plenty of rock scattered about – and his own garden. He could live there with his father. No – with Arlos. He thought about it the rest of the way.

Ava appeared in the distance walking toward him.

They met, both lost in thought, at the doorway of an imposing dwelling that reached up along the high wall of an outer path.

*

The main room of Thayn's household had been broken out to the corners several times and new walls built around them, leaving the corners to support the roof. Several looms and a great table sat in its recesses. Bristlecloth weavings hung from its walls, brightly colored, and benches and pillows defined a center space.

Zylla sat on a woven rug with three little ones. "Watch them, will you?" She handed Lo, who was the fussiest, to Ava and withdrew to the kitchen.

Thayn hurried upstairs. His room was small but cozy with a window that overlooked the adjacent outer path. He slipped out of his uniform and, wearing a fresh tunic and leggings, returned downstairs. "I'll take her." Lo crawled into Thayn's arms.

"Ava?" asked a little voice.

"Ava?" asked another.

"What?"

Neela and Zod both told her the same thing in different ways. The twins needed some help drawing a picture of their family.

Thayn's household was a complex structure. His mother, Kalia, was now married to Ava's father, Daloth. Thayn's father, Zayn, and Ava's mother, Jiara, had both taken new partners, too, Zylla and Dirak. Even Dirak and Kalia had been married briefly. Theirs was the only partnership that hadn't produced children and they all lived together. It was a precept of the city that families remain intact for the sake of siblings, step-siblings and half-siblings.

Ava had a slightly younger sister, Eril. She came to sit with them. "Let me help." Eril's bushy red hair should have made her conspicuous, but it didn't. She tended to fade into her surroundings.

"Thayn was just wonderful at tumbling," Zylla exclaimed. The women's voices carried through the household.

"Was he?"

"Oh, yes."

Ava agreed. "You should have seen him, Eril."

"I was there."

"Thayn?" His stepfather called, "Come here."

Thayn and Ava exchanged a quick look. "Yes, I'm coming."

He handed Lo to Eril and walked to a recess in the wall. Daloth sat at his loom. "Thayn. I hear you performed well. I'm pleased." *Thap foosh* went the loom.

"Thank you." Daloth married Thayn's mother after his father's so-called accident, his parent's divorce and Kalia's failed marriage to Dirak. Thayn didn't like Daloth. Only his father, Zayn, understood how special Thayn was.

Zayn sat at the nearby table, expressionless.

Daloth was older than Kalia and her former husbands, the Senior Peer of the household. He wore his thin gray hair pulled back across his baldness. *Thap foosh* went the loom.

"I'm sorry I was unable to attend. As you know," he said. *Thap foosh. Thap foosh.* Daloth smiled as if their conversation was complete.

Lo began to cry.

"Now help your sisters with the children."

Mindful of his manners, Thayn complied, glad to get away. He returned to the others on the rug. Eril handed Lo to him and she quit fussing.

*

Late afternoon yielded to early evening. Routines of the household continued and dinners were almost ready. Shadows had shifted across the marketplace to lengthen from the other side. The crowd thinned, the clamour subsided and the flapping of the banners high above in a growing wind could be heard. Boz looked out at the booths and walkways as they emptied. He wiped his countertop and smiled to himself. Another good day, thanks be to Kala.

*

Thayn went to bed early. He remembered the rewards that his father and Arlos promised him. He thought about them long into the night.

*

His eyes opened hours before dawn. "Come to me," called that undeniable voice in his head. Neither awake nor asleep, Thayn dressed in the dark. He slipped downstairs and out the front door into a stormy night. The voice led Thayn into the city.

CHAPTER THREE
The Forbidden Room

Hours later Thayn found himself in one of several reading rooms in the back of the library. "Not again." He sat at a table against the wall. Flickering oilstem was nearly spent.

Thayn walked to a window. He looked at his reflection and shrugged his shoulders. His tunic and leggings clashed, red and pink.

He rubbed his head. It hurt. He looked around at the reading room. Students rarely came here, only the most serious among them who wanted a quiet place to study. And never now.

He returned to his chair and closed his eyes. His head tilted to the side. Thayn fell, not asleep, but back into a trance.

*

On the other side of the library wall was an annex.

Few knew about it – the Forbidden Room. It housed old and tattered volumes of history and lore. Thayn's trance deepened and, in response, the covers of the old books stirred and opened. Their pages turned.

*

At dawn Jovia, the High Minister of Eator, was already at work. She left the Chamber of Ages and walked quickly through the Center. Elyda was right. Jovia had thrown the stones and it was time for a number of Choosings.

Gray hair escaped her wimple. She was older than Elyda and no less wrinkled, but there was greater vigor to Jovia and more purpose to her steps. She placed her palm to the smooth stone walls and doorways obediently opened.

She needed additional information regarding the coming moon. Jovia hurried past Thayn without noticing him on her way to the Forbidden Room.

She was preoccupied. The day would be a busy one. There were meetings that morning with delegations of Senior Peers regarding the allocation of foodstuffs. They didn't understand the appetite of the Woodswarder. And then there was a matter of some gossip among the Ministration. It must be rectified.

Jovia sighed. Order came at a price.

She entered an alcove and placed her palm to the wall. A door opened. She entered a small hallway, again placed her palm to a wall and spoke quick words. Thin light from high windows bathed the Forbidden Room.

Jovia screamed as several books snapped shut.

She emerged from the alcove a moment later, looking at the table against the wall. It was empty. Hadn't someone just been sitting there? She concentrated, attempting to sense something in the air.

*

Startled by Jovia's scream, Thayn hurried through the library. He negotiated the maze of tables and low shelves by heart, having learned his way in the dark. He bolted into the Great Path and collided with someone. They both took a step backwards.

Axl recoiled, pointing. A lick of lightning flashed overhead. He stared at Thayn with wild eyes. "You?" Axl had a ragged black beard and a mop of mottled hair.

"Oh – "

"You don't belong here," he thundered.

"Sorry, I – "

Axl hurried away, ranting to himself.

Thayn stood for a moment, shaking. He closed his

eyes. He wished that he were at home, in bed, still asleep and dreaming. He opened his eyes. He stood alone in the Great Path.

*

Thayn sat in the shadow of a broad archway that opened into the smithies. He didn't want to be early for school. Nobody would notice him here.

His stomach grumbled and he checked his book bag. Snacks. He didn't remember packing them. The last thing that he remembered was going to bed.

He decided to eat something. Other students appeared along the Great Path, yawning and laughing. Thayn watched them. He bit into a jellycrisp as Arlos walked by. His heart skipped a beat. He was going to talk to Arlos this morning. He would finally tell him how he felt.

Splat. The jellycrisp burst.

It didn't seem like such a good idea now. Jelly cleaved to his face. Luckily, Thayn knew of a public station among the smithies where he could wash up. He hurried there.

Unlike the marketplace, designed to accommodate foot traffic, the smithies were a challenge to cross. Stacks of firewood defined airy stalls that were surrounded by raw materials and goods awaiting repair.

Items already in process hung from the rafters.

Clang, clang. A few of the fires were ready. A smith hammered a broken scythe, oblivious to Thayn who dodged a shower of sparks. He continued to the wash station and entered it.

What would he say to Arlos, he wondered?

A wide basin of water sat in the corner of a simple room. After washing his face, Thayn pretended that his reflection was Arlos. "Yes, what did you want?" he asked himself.

"I just want you to know – " Thayn anticipated saying " – no – I just want to *tell* you – I just *have* to tell you – I want you to know how I *feel*." Thayn closed his eyes for a moment.

"What's this?" A burly smith entered the station.

Thayn opened his eyes and flushed. "Oh." He hurried around the man. "I was – "

He didn't finish his sentence, darting out the door and across the smithies. He entered the Great Path and joined the others on their way to school.

*

The school consisted of separate wings of classrooms, one for every nexus. A commons area connected the wings, and a lecture hall joined the school to the Center. In front were playgrounds for the younger children, and between the wings were gardens.

The walls of the school were high and wrought with skill. Their design supported instruction and the ways of Kala – purpose, utility and beauty. Architecture was precise and offered the children exemplars as they learned their lessons.

Thayn walked into the classroom of Nexus Five. Its arrangement was unfamiliar to him. Where was Arlos?

*

Jovia entered the school from the Center and hastened through the lecture hall. Something, without a doubt, had forced entry into the Forbidden Room, although she still couldn't believe her eyes. Pages were turning and then suddenly all the books closed tight. Someone, Jovia was sure, had been sitting outside as she passed. Who? A student, certainly – who else would be there? But why at that hour? Something wasn't right. She pushed a tuft of hair back into one side of her wimple.

She would sense who it was. Jovia entered the classroom of Nexus Four.

*

Arlos looked up from a table of students in the back of his classroom. "Thayn, hello," he called and hurried to join him.

"Can we talk now?"

"*Ar*-los?" called a student from the table, her voice lilting. Thayn barely heard her over the beating of his heart.

"Just a minute," Arlos promised Thayn, winking.

*

Jovia emerged from the classroom of Nexus Four. She had sensed nothing. She walked to the door of Nexus Three across from Thayn's classroom.

*

Arlos returned. "Can we meet at first bell?"

"In the garden?" Thayn pointed out the window.

Arlos shrugged. "I don't suppose we need permission, just for – "

"We don't."

"See you then." Arlos smiled.

It was a beautiful smile. "Yes."

Thayn was staring. "Thayn?"

"Oh." Thayn turned and left, hurrying through the commons into his own classroom.

*

Frowning, Jovia emerged from the classroom of Nexus Three. She went to the front wing now.

*

Thayn's classroom filled with students. It was di-
vided into smaller areas by partitions of varying height.
Those of the same age were grouped together. Ava,
dressed in red, already sat at a table assigned to her,
Rykos and Thayn. She was pouting.

"Good morning," Thayn greeted her. Immediately,
he wished that he hadn't.

"You're going to get in so much trouble. I covered
for you again. I told Kalia and Daloth – " Ava didn't
like calling their parents by name, but otherwise it was
too confusing " – I told them you had to meet with
Elyda. I lied. You're going to get in so much trouble
if you keep leaving in the morning without letting anyone know."

Thayn sighed.

Ava uncoiled her braid and refastened it hastily.
She added, "I wish I knew what you were up to."

"So do I," Thayn replied.

"What?"

"A joke." He dropped his bag on the table.

"It's not funny, Thayn."

"Sorry." He didn't sit down. Instead, he headed
for a door to outside.

"Where are you going?"

"To the garden." He looked around the room. No

teachers were watching.

"You don't have permission to – Thayn – " she called after him in frustration " – oh."

Thayn left.

*

Rykos, almost tardy after walking Aryla to Boz' booth, joined Ava at their table. He wore light blue to match his dreamy mood. "Lovely day," he said.

"Shut up."

"Where's Thayn?"

"Don't ask."

*

Thayn closed the door behind him. He stood in a leafy arbor that ran along facing wings of the school-house. A thick lawn stretched between them. Here and there slender trees stood together and spiky flowers grew everywhere.

Arlos appeared from the opposite wing. *Bong.* A single bell rang. It was a warning to students who lingered in the commons or Great Path to hurry to class. Thayn and Arlos walked toward each other and met under the trees. "Hello."

"Hi."

"You're wearing yellow again today." A simple tunic hung over Arlos' homespun leggings.

"What? Oh, yes. And you – " Arlos cocked his head as he looked at Thayn's red over pink, and finished by saying " – look like your father."

"My father?"

"I saw him yesterday, remember?"

"Oh, that's right." Thayn scrutinized Arlos, trying to imagine his face always there, by his side, as it might be in their little home in the fields.

"My parents went to school with – " Arlos hesitated " – they were friends before his accident."

"It wasn't an accident," Thayn said.

"No?"

Thayn looked away. "No, it – but that's not what I want to talk about."

"Of course," Arlos agreed. "I mean, I know what you want to talk about."

Thayn looked back quickly. Arlos' cool gray eyes seemed to look right through him. "You do? Oh – " He could barely get the words out and his heart began to race.

"We should practice together."

"We should – what?"

"Practice – tumbling. You know, practice our routines."

"Oh."

"That's what you wanted to ask me, isn't it? It makes sense."

Thayn stared at Arlos, confused. Was something wrong? Didn't Arlos feel the – *way* – he did? "I – " Thayn didn't know what to say.

"We're both good. We'll learn from each other."

Tumbling?

Wait a minute. Arlos in that uniform? It wasn't such a bad idea. "Yes. Let's – practice – together."

Arlos smiled.

Thayn took a deep breath. After a moment he added, "There's something else, though. I've been thinking lately."

"About what?" Arlos asked.

"Lots of things. Now that I'm older – I mean now that *we're* older – " Thayn stopped.

"I know what you mean."

"You do?" His heart was racing again.

"It's so confusing," Arlos admitted.

"Yes." Thayn looked into Arlos eyes. "I mean, what is?"

"The way I feel sometimes."

"How do you feel?" Thayn felt as if he were in a dream.

"Sometimes I think I know everything. And then –

I don't know – " Arlos heaved a sigh " – I feel like I'm about to burst and I get confused. Do you?"

"Yes – I mean – no. I – "

"Me, too. I wish – "

Thayn reached forward, but stopped. He wanted to touch Arlos' cheek. He reached down and picked a flower instead. It had a broad face of little petals and many colors ran through it.

"Look," Thayn said, "can you see how this pattern goes this way? And this pattern goes that way?"

"Yes."

"But they're both the *same* pattern, aren't they?"

Arlos leaned close.

"Different, but the *same*, if you get what I mean." Thayn's voice tapered to a whisper. His eyes fluttered and his lips quivered. He didn't know what to expect, but he was ready to hear anything, to do anything, as long as it was with Arlos.

"Yes, I see. Can I have it?" Arlos eyes no longer looked through him, but past him. "I'll give it to her. I'll explain it the same way."

"Her?" Thayn wasn't sure that he heard right.

"Maybe she'll understand how I feel. *Glen*-na."

"Who?"

"You know her. She's in my class." Arlos smiled.

"Well, I'd better get back. When do you want to practice?"

"What?"

"Tumbling."

Glenna?

Something was horribly wrong. "I don't know."

"All right. Well, soon, I hope. See you around. Thanks."

Thayn watched Arlos walk back across the garden and enter his wing. The door opened and a brief rush of noise escaped it. Then the garden grew quiet again.

He reached down and picked another flower.

Thayn looked at the pattern going this way and that way and he tore the flower to pieces and threw it to the ground. All his thoughts were replaced by a burning feeling.

His chin quivered. His eyes hurt. They grew hot and wet.

*

Inner paths between the public buildings of Eator were edged with tall grass. From the path that ran between the school and the auditorium Thayn could hear shouting and the slapping of feet.

Woodswarder?

CHAPTER FOUR
Beyond the Wooden Wall

Woodswarder were seldom seen in the city. They approached more quickly than Thayn thought possible. He could hear voices now, two – no, three – of them. He scrambled to the hedge and pulled the grass aside. Wiping his eyes, he watched.

Their haste was obvious. They hadn't waited on robes, wearing their bristlecloth pulled up through their belts at the front and back. Two bristlecloth were green, the color of Eator. The third was gray.

Thayn ran along the inside of the grassy hedge. The Woodswarder bounded up the steps to the Center. The Woodsward in gray steadied himself, breathing hard, as the others pounded on the smooth stone wall.

Woodswarder were men of legend and exaggeration. Thayn looked up at them through the plumes of grass. The nostrils of the Woodsward in gray flared and his eyes darted. Crusty gashes covered his calves and still bled.

"Oh – " Thayn caught an exclamation of surprise in his throat. Did they hear him? Had they seen him? He didn't think so.

The wall opened. The Woodswarder disappeared and it closed again.

Thayn stared at the Center for a moment. Nothing happened. He listened, particularly in the direction of the path, tilting his head. He was known to have keen ears, but Thayn heard nothing more.

Feeling a surge of vulnerability, he turned and ran across the garden as fast as he could. He opened his classroom door.

He closed it again quickly, all but a sliver, and peered through the crack. Jovia stood across the room, her eyes closed. Elyda stood next to her. They scrutinized the students.

Bong. Bong. Ding. Thayn turned and looked up. Bells in the Center rang. *Bong. Bong. Ding.* It was a call to High Council.

Thayn opened the door again.

Jovia was leaving. Elyda was talking to Yara. Then Elyda left, too.

Thayn slipped back into the room and returned to

their table.

"There you are," Rykos welcomed him.

"What's going on?" Thayn sat down.

Ava was reading and still pouting. She didn't look up from her book.

Thayn looked at her, then at Rykos.

Rykos shrugged.

"I can tell you're not reading, Ava," Thayn said at last. "Your lips aren't moving."

Ava slammed her book shut. "I covered for you again. Elyda came by with our assignments. I told her you dropped your notebook and went looking for it."

"Thanks."

"Forget it." Ava snorted.

"I'm sorry."

"I don't like telling lies."

"I didn't ask you to lie." Thayn wasn't interested in fighting with Ava right now, but her remark bothered him. "If you don't want to lie, say you don't know. Or don't say anything at all. I didn't ask you to, did I? Did I say, 'Ava, I'm going out in the garden, if Elyda comes by, lie for me, will you?'"

"What about this morning?"

"I – "

"Children, children," Rykos admonished them.

"Anyway – " Thayn looked across the partitioned classroom to the windows. He couldn't see the entrance to the Center from here, so Ava and Rykos, he decided, couldn't have seen anything, either.

"Who dressed you, by the way?" Rykos asked.

Thayn ignored him. " – I want to tell you something." He sat down again.

"Thayn," Ava complained, "you're acting weird."

"Just now out in the garden I saw – "

"Good morning." Yara joined them. After nodding at Thayn and Rykos, she gazed at Ava and her round face became beautiful.

Thayn coughed. Yara wasn't aware that she interrupted him.

Rykos sat back in his chair.

Ava sat forward and brightened.

"Good morning," they replied.

"Elyda had to go to High Council. She asked me to make sure you had your readings and assignments."

"Yes."

"Oh, yes."

"Do you need any help?"

Rykos winked at Thayn. "This part, maybe. The realizations of Kala."

"What about them?" Yara asked.

"I don't understand any of it. 'And by making many of one, Kala made one of many, and the transformation began.'"

"Yes. And then?"

"Then?" Rykos scratched his chin.

"What happens next?" Yara coaxed him.

"What happens? I get confused, that's what happens next."

Ava rolled her eyes.

"Now," Rykos suggested, "if it said, 'and the *confusion* began,' *that* would make sense."

Thayn laughed.

"Oh," Ava complained. "Rykos, listen. Kala had *all*, right, *everything*, but not *anything*, because it was only *one* thing, so from it he made *many*."

"That's right. You're in capable hands." Yara left, smiling.

"So, how could he not have – *any*thing?" Rykos shook his head. "If he had *everything*? And why is *many* different from *one* if it's all made from the same stuff – ?"

"You're missing the point." Ava looked at him sharply.

Rykos closed his book and pushed it away. "I'm ready to go to the fields."

"You don't know if you'll go to the fields," Ava objected.

"But I want to."

"Oh, I'm fed up with both of you. Until your Choosings you have to prepare for everything."

"I know what you're preparing for," Rykos countered.

"What?"

"Bossing people around."

"I – no, I'm not." Ava evidently forgot that she was mad at Thayn and appealed to him in defense. "Thayn?"

Here was Thayn's chance to make peace, but he was thinking about the Woodswarder. He wanted to tell Ava and Rykos what he saw.

Ding. Ding. Ding. The students looked up. A single bell rang. *Ding. Ding. Ding.* It didn't stop. They looked around.

"Curfew," Ava whispered.

"What?"

"It's a call to curfew." Never in their lifetimes had curfew been called in Eator.

"How do you know?" Rykos asked.

Pushing it back to him, Ava said, "It's in your book."

A stocky Monitor in a green hooded robe entered the classroom and spoke with Yara. Yara addressed the class.

"Students, please return quickly to your nexus. Do so in an orderly fashion. You have your assignments. Older students, please assist your brothers and sisters. Hurry now, home."

Ava charged them, "Rykos, help Thayn with Eril, Neela and Zod. Not all the younger children have older brothers and sisters. *Ya*-ra needs me." Ava left the table.

Ding. Ding. Ding. Rykos and Thayn stood up. "You heard her," Rykos said. "Let's do as we're told."

The younger children were in different areas of the wing. Thayn found Eril by her bushy red hair. He told her, "Go with Rykos and get Neela. I'll get Zod and meet you in the commons room."

Zod was at a difficult age. He didn't understand that anything serious was happening and ran away from Thayn several times. "Come on, you little monster." Zod laughed.

They were last to leave the classroom. Ava stood with Yara and the teachers in the commons surrounded by younger students. They would escort them home. Eril, Neela and Rykos waited for Thayn and Zod.

They left the school and hurried along the Great Path, passing the auditorium. No Senior Peers lingered in its breezeways. *Ding. Ding. Ding.*

The adjacent temple was empty, too. With the incessant clanging of the bell, prayers became personal. Many were offered under the breath.

Across the Great Path from the temple, the Fallow Field remained unaffected by the unexpected course of events. Uninhabited by the living – and untended – it was overgrown with flowering herbs. Upon them were scattered the ashes of the dead.

*

They arrived home. Their parents and the little ones sat together in the middle of the room. "Here are Thayn and Neela and Zod. Good."

"And here comes Eril. Join us, all of you."

"Where's Ava?" Daloth asked. His face was thin and serious.

"She's helping Yara with the younger children," Thayn replied.

Daloth looked carefully from parent to parent. He squinted at Thayn and the children. The bell stopped.

The children all asked different questions at the same time. Daloth silenced them with the wave of his hand. Although not great in stature, his presence was commanding. "Work on your assignments."

They complained, but Daloth raised an eyebrow. They hushed.

Eril helped Zod and Neela with their books. Then she read, too. The women rocked the little ones in their arms. Daloth and Dirak sat together and spoke in brief whispers. Zayn stared off into space.

Thayn was too distracted to read. He opened his notebook and absently began to draw. He closed his eyes. Events of the day flooded his thinking. Waking up in the library. His conversation with Arlos. The arrival of the Woodswarder.

His drawing took shape. Thayn opened his eyes again. Lately, his drawings were always the same.

*

Elyda followed Jovia down the aisle of the lecture hall and across a small stage. A palm to the wall and a doorway opened into the ancient stone Center, home of the Ministration. Compared to the public buildings of Eator, wrought with precision and care, to say nothing of the more spontaneous dwellings of the Genexus, the Center was singular in its grace and simplicity. None of Eator, living or dead, possessed the knowledge and power to erect such an edifice. It was attributable only to Kala himself.

A seamless stone hallway ran inside its circumference. From it branched other passageways that led deep into the Center. Overhead vents offered light by day and, by night, served as flues for oilstem.

The doors of the High Chamber opened at Jovia's touch and closed behind them. She and Elyda took respective places behind a curved dais beside five other women of the High Council.

A Ministrant brought robes for the waiting Woodswarder. "We won't delay with formality," Jovia said as soon as she and Elyda were in place.

The Woodsward in gray stepped forward. His hair was scaled with sweat. "Thank you." He daubed his face with the sleeve of his robe.

"State your business."

His pain was too profound for him to share in words. Instead, he communicated in thought. "Yutor has been attacked. We've been destroyed."

"By whom?"

"I don't know."

"When?"

"Two nights ago."

"Your defenses – how did they fail?"

The Woodsward spoke aloud now, his obvious restraint measuring greater frustration. "They came from *within* the city."

"How is this possible?"

"There was no alarm," the Woodsward continued. "No battle. We were slain in the Ring, many of us in our sleep. I stand here without pride."

"Your Ministration?"

"I don't know."

Jovia concentrated. After a moment she shook her head. "I'm unable to find your High Minister in my thoughts – oh." She flinched.

Members of the High Council closed their eyes. Among them a silent dialogue ensued.

Jovia announced at last, "A curfew. The city will stand on alert. Alarms will sound in response to any ir-regularity. And I must convoke the Senior Peers."

Their eyes opened.

Jovia looked at Elyda. "You don't agree?"

"It will frighten the Genexus," Elyda asserted. It was a continual controversy, how much information to share with them.

"They need to know." Jovia returned her attention to the Woodsward from Yutor. "Your name?"

"Kaden." He held his jaw firm.

"Welcome, Kaden, to Eator. Your city, should you choose."

"An honor. Yet – " He furrowed his brow, hesitating.

Jovia concluded softly, "You will do what is best. You can do nothing more." She raised her palm and the doors of the High Chamber opened.

*

The Woodswarder returned to the hall that ran inside the circumference of the Center. They would travel by a different path directly to the camp of the High Warden. After his report, Kaden would be made welcome to the Ring.

A prim Ministrant awaited the Woodswarder at the appointed door. "The robes are yours to keep." The wall opened at her touch and the Woodswarder departed the Center, this time passing between the temple and the marketplace.

*

The High Council concluded. Jovia stood. "Leave me," she requested.

The other women obeyed.

Jovia remained alone at the dais. She held a hand to her head and clenched her fingers. "No – " Her cry was cut short. Although her lips continued to move, no sound escaped them.

She collapsed.

*

Most of the Genexus were already in their homes. The marketplace was empty. Hooded Monitors tended the smithies' fires. Ava had seen the last of her group of students home from school and hurried past the statuary bordering the Fallow Field.

Ahead three Monitors ran across the Great Path. A hood slipped and Ava almost cried aloud. Woodswarder? She ducked among the statues of former High Ministers and they didn't see her.

*

Thayn's household remained silent. The little ones slept in their mothers' arms, except Lo who wiggled about on the rug. The men dozed, too. "No, Lo," Eril scolded her. She and the twins did schoolwork on the rug. Thayn watched his father. He was seemingly oblivious to everything that was happening around them. Was his father, Thayn wondered, despite all that he endured, the lucky one?

His musing was interrupted by the faint sound of foot upon stone. No one else seemed to hear. It came through his bedroom window from the outer path. The footfall grew louder.

Thayn recognized the sound. It was the Woodswarder. He closed his notebook. He felt a surge of

54

excitement and, without realizing it, scrambled to his feet.

Daloth opened his eyes. Thayn froze. He adjusted his leggings, as if that were his intent.

He heard voices now, too. Only because his step-father scowled at him did Thayn resist the impulse to run upstairs. The Woodswarder passed. Thayn tilted his head, listening as their footsteps faded. He sat down again.

Ava burst through the door, flushed and excited. "I'm – "

They all looked up at her, startled, except for Dirak, who yawned.

" – home," she announced. Jiara gestured for her to sit beside her.

"I'm glad," Daloth replied in a concluding tone.

They continued to sit in silence.

Ava glanced at Thayn. She wanted nothing more than to tell him about the Woodswarder, not knowing that he wanted to do the same.

Abruptly the bells rang again. *Bong. Ding. Bong.* Everyone looked up.

It was a call to the Senior Peers, a call to convo-cation. Daloth spoke softly with Dirak for a moment, then aloud to everyone else. "Until I return, curfew continues." Nobody dared to complain. He smoothed his tunic and hurried out the door.

Dirak wasn't as strict as Daloth. Ava joined Thayn on the rug and they began to whisper. "I saw Woodswarder just now."

"I heard them. I saw them earlier."

"Where?"

"In the garden."

"Why didn't you tell me?"

"You were mad at me, remember?"

"I'm still mad at you. Why do you suppose they're here?"

Thayn shrugged and leafed through his notebook.

"Truce?" Ava capitulated.

"Truce." Thayn smiled

"What's that?" she inquired, looking at his drawing.

"Nothing." She reached over and ripped it out.

"No," Thayn objected too loudly.

Dirak looked up. Unlike Daloth who would separate them for even a perceived transgression of his will, they knew that Dirak would do nothing unless they provoked him. Thayn and Ava ignored each other until, again, Dirak dozed.

Ava whispered, "Where did you get this?"

"I drew it."

She examined it again. "It looks like a body."

"It's a map."

"Of what?"

"The land, I think."

"A map of the body of the land? A map of Kala? Thayn, that's Forbidden Knowledge."

"How do you know?"

"Dirak? May Thayn and I go sit at the big table? We need to work on our project and we'd hate to disturb Eril." Eril only pretended to read. Instead, both Thayn and Ava knew, she listened to their conversation.

Dirak stirred and nodded. Eril looked up from her book and stuck out her tongue.

*

Thayn and Ava had been classmates longer than they had been stepbrother and stepsister. After his so-called accident Zayn couldn't head the household. He and Kalia divorced and she and Dirak married. Despite his good nature, they were ill-suited. Kalia found comfort in Daloth who lived nearby with his unhappy wife, Jiara, and their daughters, Ava and Eril.

Dirak and Jiara found themselves to be a better match. Daloth and his family joined the household, but now Daloth and Kalia, and Dirak and Jiara, were partners.

Zylla came as nurse to Zayn. Instead they married, too. Thayn resented many of the changes, but he never talked about it.

Some things remained the same, though. He and Ava were always friends. Eril wasn't, really. She was just Ava's sister, his stepsister.

*

Thayn and Ava moved to a broad wooden table that sat in a cozy alcove. It was usually reserved for meals. Ava finally answered Thayn's question. "This morning I overheard Jovia say something about the Forbidden Room."

"What's that?"

"I asked Yara about it. She said it's full of old books and incantations – and *maps of Kala* – stuff like that. She swore me to secrecy."

"Where is this place, the Forbidden Room?"

"In the back of the library."

Thayn's eyes widened. "That's where I wake up sometimes."

"What?"

"When you cover for me. I leave in the middle of the night and wake up in the back of the library."

"Why?"

"I don't know."

"Let's ask Yara."

"No."

"There has to be a reason why you go there."

"Ava – " Thayn hesitated. "Do you ever hear a voice in your head?"

"Like your conscience?"

"I guess so."

"A voice that tells you right from wrong?"

Dirak called from the next room. "Ava? Thayn? Are you studying?"

"Yes, we are." They sat for a moment in silence.

"There's something I've never told you." Thayn hesitated. "Something I've never told anybody."

"What?"

"Years ago, before you – joined us – "

Ava flushed. She, too, resented the changes that they shared.

" – one of the neighbors was ill," he continued, "and mother was staying with her."

"Yes."

"There's a drawer in this table."

"I know."

"It used to be out there, the table, before – " he

59

pointed into the main room.

"Thayn, you're rambling."

"One night when Mother wasn't here, I heard noises. Father was sitting – here – at the table," Thayn gestured, remembering. "He pulled the drawer out. Lots of old books were piled up – there. He tore a page out of one of them and stuck it under the drawer. He replaced it just as Monitors came through the door."

"Monitors?"

"And Jovia."

"Jovia? Here?"

"Not so loud."

Ava glanced into the next room. "Let's look in the appendix," she suggested, making sure that everyone, especially Dirak, could hear her. She opened her book to the back and whispered, "Then what?"

"They got in an argument. About the books. Jovia said he shouldn't have them. Father's face had expression then. He looked like – me. They argued more. He shouted at Jovia. Then he held his hands to his forehead. His face got ugly.

"He pointed at her. She held up her palm. Suddenly he slumped over.

"Jovia looked scared. 'I didn't do this,' she said a

60

couple of times. The Monitors took the books. They all left. I don't think they saw me. Father has been – this way – ever since."

Ava looked at Thayn. "Why didn't you ever tell me?"

"He said not to."

"Who?"

"Father. He talks to me – in my head. We go out for walks together. Sometimes I wake up places and I don't know how I got there."

With another glance into the next room Ava pulled the drawer from the table. She lifted it up, extracted a piece of paper from under its runner and unfolded it.

Ava's eyes grew wide as she realized what she held. "A map of the Center."

"What?"

A maze of chambers and hallways was painstakingly depicted. The High Chamber, the Hall of Choosing, private areas assigned to the High Minister and other members of the Ministration. Everything clearly labeled. On the back were illustrations of the Doors of Choosings and other detail.

"Thayn, this is serious."

CHAPTER FIVE
Madness

The three Woodswarder took broad strides along the outer path. The walls lowered after they passed the dwellings of the Genexus. To one side gardens and tracts of bristle were well-tended. To the other side the Fallow Field grew in tangles of flowering herb.

Accompanying Kaden were Tylos, a captain, and Owan, the sector scout who first spotted Kaden's arrival. Events had played out quickly. It was decided that they would report immediately to High Council. Now the Woodswarder returned.

The day was warm. Tylos pulled off his hooded robe. Normally on visits to the city Woodswarder requested robes in advance in order to disguise themselves as Monitors, but today their business had been urgent. As curfew continued, Tylos reasoned that their appearance was of no concern. The others followed his example. According to custom they secured their bristlecloth through woven belts at their side.

"A moment," Tylos said. The men stopped. They were all broad at the shoulder, triangular torsos on slim hips.

Tylos' hair was black and fell in braids down his back. Owan was fairer and, despite a well-muscled frame, seemed softer than his companions. Kaden, severe in his countenance, was blistered by the sun and blotched with blood and sweat. "Homage awaits you both. Let me express mine now," Tylos continued.

He took each of Owan's shoulders by a hand and kissed him gently on the forehead. "You have sharp eyes." They were brown and flecked with yellow.

Owan smiled.

To Kaden, "My new friend, welcome. You've endured much." Tylos knelt on one knee. He kissed Kaden, too.

As they continued on their way, Tylos could hear Kaden's thoughts. "I should have fought."

"Only to die?" Tylos asked. They communicated without words.

"Perhaps," Kaden replied in thought.

"Would it have been easier?"

Kaden considered. "Perhaps," he repeated.

Tylos shook his head. "You're not a coward. And worse than a coward is a fool."

*

Daloth walked with several other Senior Peers down the Great Path to convocation. Some of them had just returned to their homes from the fields, the marketplace and the smithies for curfew and now they were called away again. It would take time for everybody to arrive.

Senior Peers already entered the auditorium. Daloth was surprised that none stood knotted in conversation in the breezeways outside its doors. He asked aloud, "Have they started without us?

"Impossible." A curve of tiered stone seats faced an ornate stage. Only a few Senior Peers had taken their usual places. The rest stood clogging the aisles.

All attention was focused on Jovia who, at the podium, stood like a wild creature. Her wimple was torn at the crown and she tugged at her hair. It came out in her hands. Other Ministration tried to pull her away but she fought them off, kicking them.

She looked out in the direction of the Senior Peers, her eyes rolling in their sockets. "Stop it," she wailed, warning them all. "It must be stopped."

A concerted effort by the Ministration removed her

from the podium. She struggled again at the wall to the Center.

It opened. Jovia howled as they pushed her into waiting arms. The wall closed behind her.

The Senior Peers stood speechless. They looked at the remaining Ministration. The remaining Ministration looked among themselves. Finally, with obvious reluctance, Elyda approached the podium. By doing so, she assumed temporary leadership of the city.

"Go home. Be wary. I will call you together again tomorrow afternoon. First, there is much I must learn." She turned and left the auditorium through the same door as Jovia.

*

The Woodswarder reached the Wooden Wall. Except for hidden gates, it was formed by living trees. The trunks pressed together and grew around one another, impenetrable. Tylos hailed the guards.

Kaden detected no interruption among the trees until their trunks parted. Here the world of the Ministration and Genexus ended. They stepped through the gate into the Ring of the Woodswarder.

It was a great, green vault. A thick canopy began at the Wooden Wall and arched high. Gradually the ceiling lowered again, tapering to smaller trees and stands of scrub and fern to meet the outside world. It formed a membrane around the city.

The Ring wasn't known to the Genexus for what it really was, nor did many of them choose to think of a world beyond the Wooden Wall. Genexus were taught that they lived within a vast forest. The Woodswarder protected them.

Kaden scanned the leafy ceiling. Fluttering green-golden light offered a reassuring sky. These were unfamiliar trees and strangers stood in them, but their sight and smell, their very feel, comforted him.

A steward awaited them and Tylos withdrew. The steward led Kaden and Owan to a nearby wash station. They made ready for audience with the High Warden.

*

Kaden appeared more relaxed after a welcome visit to the wash station. His hair fell freely about sun-burned shoulders. Smoothed with unguent, he gleamed like bronze. Owan emerged moments later flushed and creamy pink. Fresh bristlecloth hung at their sides.

The steward escorted Kaden and Owan through an understory of bushes and ferns to a great clearing, the High Camp of Eator. In the middle of the clearing a stand of ancient gnarlwood formed a small pavilion.

Owan and Kaden entered, squinting against a contrast of shimmering light and shadow. Around a hewn log six captains of the Woodswarder, each representing a sector of the Ring, sat on either side of the High Warden. Tylos was among them.

Kaden and Owan knelt.

The High Warden was Cyrll. He nodded at his captains and they grew quiet. He dismissed the steward.

Kaden scrutinized Cyrll. He was massive, a powerful man, but his manner was gentle. Little older than Kaden himself, his hair was white. He wore on his head a withered wreath. Kaden sensed in him immeasurable contradiction.

Cyrll stood, his thick arms branching, his torso as solid as the trunk of any tree. He held his hands low and to his side. His palms opened.

Kaden felt Cyrll find his mind. He heard Cyrll's thinking. Kaden stood. They spent a moment in silent communication.

Owan wasn't a communicator. He looked at them uncomprehendingly.

Cyrll plucked a purple berry from a sprig that appeared at his fingertips. He still held Kaden in his gaze. "Approach me," he thought. Kaden walked to the hewn log and, in communion with his host, knelt again. Now the berry lay on Kaden's tongue.

Cyrll turned his attention to Owan, opening the young scout's mind. Owan suddenly knew things of which he had been unaware. The true scope of Yutor's devastation. The extent of Kaden's despair. The uncertainty of his heart.

Owan, too, was offered a berry. The men chewed. The berries burst. Juice stained their lips.

Stewards brought pillows and a feast of fruit and baked goods. Cyrll's captains visited quietly together, their business concluded. Kaden reclined, Owan at his side, and blinked. The juice of the berries offered both immediate calm and invigoration.

Entertainment commenced. Several Woodswarder fell from high in the trees and twirled through the air. Kaden narrowed his eyes. Aerialists. They sailed in and out of focus.

Kaden was made welcome to the Ring of Eator.

*

Daloth returned from convocation sooner than anyone expected, especially Thayn and Ava. The map of the Center was securely under the drawer again, but they hadn't time to decide what to do next.

"May we go outside and play now?" Zod asked.

"Not today."

"Was convocation cancelled?" Jiara asked.

"Come, everyone," Daloth called. Thayn and Ava hurried to join the others. They expected that Daloth would have some news related to the Woodswarder. Instead, he announced, "Jovia is ill."

"What?"

"Madness has taken her."

"How horrible."

"Elyda stands in her place."

"Elyda?" several of them whispered. Thayn and Ava exchanged glances.

"We will meet with her again tomorrow." Daloth described convocation. Thayn wanted to ask a question, but Ava shook her head. Daloth would offer more information if left to his loquacious nature. He described the incident with Jovia in detail and went on to relate comments made by fellow Senior Peers.

Thayn couldn't repress his objections. "It doesn't make sense," he blurted out at last. "Jovia was in our classroom when the bell rang for High Council."

"What of it?" Daloth frowned, making it clear that he had been interrupted.

"She was fine. Didn't she say anything else?"

Daloth closed his eyes for a moment. He didn't like to be questioned.

"She didn't mention any – ?"

" – other business of the city?" Ava interceded.

Daloth smiled insincerely. "I've told you what I heard. I've given my report according to my station. Even so – business of the city isn't your – responsibility." The edge to his voice was keen.

"Thayn, come sit by me," Kalia suggested.

"Ava," Jiara called.

"Let's discuss what we know," Daloth lectured them. "We know there is bristle to be dyed. There is bristle to be carded and spun. There is bristle to be woven. There is food to be prepared. There are children to be tended.

"There is plenty we *do* know and plenty for us to *do* without resorting to pointless conjecture. We prepare best for the future by doing our best in the present, and we prepare better for the unknown by doing our best with what we know.

"Ava, you will assist your mother with the vats. Eril, you will card and, Thayn, you will spin. Kalia and Zylla, the children are your charge. Dirak and I will weave.

"As we work, I want you all to contemplate our activity. We work separately, but we work together. We take what we are given, bristle, fruit and grain, and children, and with intent and effort we make something out of them, something better.

"As we work I want all to pray to Kala for the welfare of Jovia. She, better than any of us, better than us all, perhaps, understands only through our intent and effort may we avoid the many things that would take from us the simple world we enjoy.

"Let's begin." Daloth walked to his loom. *Thap foosh. Thap foosh.* Harmony was an essential component of the household compact. Everyone did as Daloth directed.

*

For Thayn and Ava the rest of the day was miserable. Ava and her mother dyed bristle at the hearth. Jiara, as requested, prayed to Kala, whispering as they worked. As the vats were set to steep, they joined the others at the table.

After a brief noon repast, Ava drained and rinsed the bristle. Its hulls separated from sodden clumps of bright color, red, yellow and orange. She spread the bristle on woven racks to dry.

Bristle produced an inconsistent filament. As a result the Genexus were constantly at work producing clothing that too easily fell apart. Far more effort was spent on its color and pattern than on its durability. In

71

the greater scheme of things, perhaps, bristlecloth provided the Genexus sustained purpose, but Ava hated
attending to the vats. It was hot and smelly work.

Thayn, meanwhile, sat in one of the smaller al-
coves and spun bristle from earlier lots as thinly as he
dared. If spun too coarse it would jam his stepfathers'
looms. Too thin and it would break. Spinning was
boring work, but it required his full attention. Piles of
bristle, already carded by Eril, waited.

*

Dinner consisted of herbed bread, a type of stalk
that Thayn didn't much enjoy, and redfruit. Daloth
asked everyone at the table to share their prayers for
Jovia. Thayn and Ava scrambled to think of something
to say but, by the time their elders had finished, dinner
was over. "Let's resume our work," Daloth said.

*

Ava turned the bristle as it dried. Thayn spun.
Left to themselves, working separately, they wished
that they could share their thoughts with each other.
They reviewed various details of the day regarding
Jovia, maps and drawings, the Forbidden Room and
the Woodswarder.

Then Ava thought about Yara.

Thayn thought about Arlos. He would tumble with

Arlos, yes. It was a good idea. "Then Arlos won't think about Glenna anymore."

He finished his spinning. The others completed their tasks and Daloth said good night. His announcement indicated that the evening was over. The family prepared for bed and Thayn hurried upstairs.

*

A benefit of the household size was the recent second story. Thayn's own room afforded him welcome privacy. He pulled off his tunic and leggings.

Moonlight poured through the window. Thayn watched the outer path awhile, too excited to sleep. Finally, he crawled into bed.

Memories of the day flooded him. Arlos. The Woodswarder. He closed his eyes. His spindle floated in front of him. Thayn drifted, exploring his thoughts.

At last, he slept. His dreams continued where his thoughts and memories left off.

*

Thayn heard a voice calling him. Was it, as Ava had suggested, his conscience?

CHAPTER SIX

The stones are thrown

It was his mother's voice. "Thayn. You'll be late for school."

"What?" He had overslept. Thayn sprang out of bed, pausing only long enough to consider what to wear, green leggings and a purple tunic.

He hurried downstairs. Ava, Eril and the twins, colorfully dressed, waited by the door. Thayn grabbed his bag and they hurried off to school, negotiating the most direct path among the crooked walkways. Still Thayn and Ava couldn't talk together as they liked. Eril refused to be excluded again, walking between them. Ava adjusted Eril's collar. "Quit it."

"Your collar is crooked," Ava said.

"I'm old enough to dress myself, thank you." She declined her head in an odd fashion as she spoke.

Thayn switched to Ava's other side.

Eril squeezed between them again. "Remember, on my birthday I'm just as old as you."

It was hard to believe – but true. Eril was born on the eve of Ava's first birthday, and too soon. Her birth was premature and she almost died. She was smaller than Ava and often sickly. Thayn tried to be sympathetic, but sometimes it just seemed to him that Eril wanted attention.

"I'm not a child," Eril continued. They walked all the way to the Great Path in silence. Suddenly sincere, she asked, "Should we be scared?"

Ava glanced at Thayn. Was she serious? Or just being Eril?

"Are you scared?" Ava asked.

"A little."

Thayn looked at Neela and Zod. They ran ahead of them. So young, they barely knew who Jovia was. "I'm not going to be scared," Ava decided.

She and Thayn would have to talk later. Ava reached for Eril's collar again. This time Eril let her pull it and smooth it down.

*

They arrived at school and entered the commons. Yara stood with several teachers at the back of the room. Elyda joined them.

"Thayn?" called an unwelcome voice.

Thayn turned. Edos, Miara and Weela approached, themselves brightly dressed. "You have hurt Miara's feelings."

"Edos, no," Miara complained.

Weela giggled.

"I said I was sorry."

"She didn't believe you."

"Yes, I did," Miara protested.

"You didn't mean it," Edos accused Thayn.

Thayn took a deep breath. The voice in his head asked him, "You've had about enough of this, haven't you?"

Yes, Thayn agreed. He was tired of being on the receiving end of things.

"I'm sorry, all right." Thayn walked right up to Edos, pushing against him with his fingertips. "I'm sorry I have to deal with you making trouble where there isn't any."

"But – "

"If you have a problem, it's yours, not mine. Now leave me alone." Thayn turned and headed for his classroom.

He heard a loud *thwack* and turned back around. Ava rubbed her hand and Edos rubbed his cheek. His cheek was red and everyone's eyes were wide.

Thayn hadn't seen the disrespectful gesture that Edos made after he turned away, but Ava saw it. She slapped him. Nobody anticipated the transformation that came over Weela. "How dare you?" She stepped forward and took a swing at Ava.

"Weela, no." Miara pulled her away.

Rykos had just come through the door and ran to them. "Ava, are you all right?"

Thayn felt a hand on his shoulder. It belonged to Elyda. "Come with me, all of you."

Yara accompanied them. They went to one of several offices in the front of the school. Edos, Miara and Weela glared at Thayn, Ava, and Rykos while Elyda and Yara whispered together. "Go." Yara left, closing the door behind her.

Before Elyda could say another word, the students all spoke at once. "She slapped him," Miara protested, pointing to Ava.

"He insulted her." Edos pointed at Thayn.

"You insulted him," Ava countered. "I saw you."

"I didn't do anything," Thayn maintained.

"You did," Weela objected.

"Your timing could not be worse," Elyda sighed, speaking more to herself than to them. "However, this

77

is something that *can* be done."

"Dut," Rykos complained, glaring at Edos.

"I resent – whatever that means – and – "

"As you may know by now," Elyda interrupted, "I'm currently High Minister of the city."

The students grew quiet.

"Your stones have been thrown. It's time for your Choosings."

Again they all spoke at once. "What?"

"At last."

"Our Choosings?"

"When?"

Elyda replied, "Your examinations will be tomorrow morning."

"Tomorrow?" Their jaws dropped.

"I'm sure you'll all do well. Ceremonies begin at noon. I'll release you now to inform your parents – and to study – and see you here again in the morning. Dismissed."

*

As Thayn and the others left the room, Yara returned with the rest of the older students. Arlos looked excited – but he didn't look at Thayn.

Yara paused to congratulate Ava. "I'll explain to Eril you've left early. Now go."

*

Edos didn't bother Thayn now. He, Miara and Weela, talking among themselves, entered the Great Path. Ava glanced at them. "Let's go this way." She, Thayn and Rykos walked in the opposite direction.

Rykos walked backwards and shared his thoughts as quickly as they came into his head. "I wonder what it'll be like. What if I can't decide? I mean, I know what my decision is, but what if I don't think the right thoughts, or what if – ?"

"It doesn't work that way, Rykos," Ava said.

"You've made your choice – or it's made you – already," Thayn agreed, smiling, remembering Aryla in the marketplace.

"Besides, the stones are overdue," Ava added. "Father – I mean, Daloth, taught me – "

" – how to tell time by the moon, we know."

"It's true."

They walked for a few moments in silence before Rykos resumed musing, "What if it's like when I really want leafcake, but the honey dumplings look good, too? Wouldn't it be horrible to make a mistake? Especially when you already know?"

Thayn only half-listened now, silently reviewing everything that he knew about Choosings. It wasn't much. The most definitive moment in a lifetime, and nobody spoke about it. A lot of what he knew he had learned in the back room of the library.

In no time they reached the archway of their nexus. "I'm glad we're off early," Ava remarked.

"Really?" Rykos asked. "I thought you liked being kept after school."

"What do you mean by – ?" Rykos was still walking backwards ahead of them, but he went the wrong way. Ava interrupted herself, "Where are you going?"

"My parents aren't home yet. I'm in the mood for something sweet." Rykos entered the marketplace.

Thayn laughed.

"You're supposed to go *find* your parents and tell them," Ava called after him.

"Ava? Thayn? What are you doing here?" Kalia was on her way home from the smithies with a mended bucket. Foot traffic and carts on the Great Path worked their way around them as they talked.

Thayn didn't fully realize his excitement until he shared the news with his mother. "Elyda met with us. The stones have been thrown. It's time for our Choosings."

Kalia's deep green eyes closed, then opened again, liquid. She extended her hand and Thayn held it. She hugged him, and Ava, too. "I'm so proud. When will they be?"

"Tomorrow," Thayn told her.

"So soon?"

"They're overdue," Ava explained.

"Yes, your father has said as much," Kalia replied. "We must have a party tonight," she added quickly.

"Our examination is in the morning," Ava said.

"We must have a party anyway."

The examination. Thayn's heart skipped a beat. He wished that Ava had reminded Rykos of it before he left for Boz' booth.

*

Once home, Ava informed her father and mother. "We'll have a party," Jiara affirmed.

"Yes," Kalia agreed.

"The stones are overdue," Daloth declared. "I've said as much."

Jiara and Kalia laughed. Then they wept.

Zylla returned from the marketplace with several bags of foodstuffs, bread and fruit, enough for tomorrow, she thought. All of it would go on the table that night. She let out a cry at the news and hugged Jiara and Kalia tightly, and Daloth softly. After checking on the little ones she returned, her cheeks wet, and hugged

Ava and Thayn. "I almost forgot you."

*

Dirak and Zayn returned. Their buckets were full of mushrooms.

*

Kaden awoke early that morning with a start. Where was he? The pavilion was a pool of checkered light. Memories flooded him.

He was in Eator, yes. He had delivered his report. There was nothing left to do but surrender to grief. He sat with his head in his hands.

Owan entered the pavilion and squinted for a moment as his eyes adjusted. Kaden composed himself, squaring his jaw.

"Good morning." Owan carried a tray of fruit and bread and set it down. His brown eyes were warm and excited. "Cyrll invites you to explore the Ring and find a home in it." His greeting sounded memorized.

"Thank you." Kaden ignored the tray. His eyes were cool and distant. He was distracted by thoughts more real than the present.

"I've offered myself as your guide," Owan continued breathlessly. His enthusiasm was genuine.

"That won't be necessary." Kaden left the pavilion. Owan followed, trailing him to the wash station and waiting outside. Kaden emerged at last, refreshed, and leapt into the trees. Their branches were broad and well-knit. No portion of the canopy was incomplete. The Ring hid the city from the land, and itself from the city.

Occasional bridging was required to provide various pathways through the trees. Kaden made his way at random, looking now and again over his shoulder. Owan lagged behind him. Ahead of them was the Wooden Wall.

*

Two Genexus dressed in yellow and orange wandered far out into the fields early that morning. Sunshine splashed against the shadows. The men hunted mushrooms, looking among stumps and saplings. The man in yellow found several clumps, filled his basket and discovered more. He called to the other Genexus.

Slowly, the man in orange approached.

*

Pushing aside a branch, Kaden watched the Genexus. "That man – " he hissed.

Owan appeared at Kaden's side. "Yes?"

"What's he doing here?"

"Hunting mushrooms, I think."

"You don't understand. I need to know who he

83

is." Owan looked at him uncomprehendingly. Frustrated, Kaden decided, "I need to see Tylos. Where is he?"

"In his tower," Owan said, pointing. "I'll take you to him."

*

Again Kaden ran along an outer path to the Center of the city. This time he already wore a hooded robe – the sector gates had been stocked with them – and was accompanied by the High Warden himself.

*

Thayn heard a banging at the door. Zylla opened it. "Oh."

Hooded Monitors entered the household. Thayn was sure that they had come for him. Everyone grew quiet and glanced at one another.

The Monitors looked from the buckets of mushrooms to the men's tunics. One of them pointed at Zayn and another said, "Come with us."

Daloth took a step forward. "See here – "

"It's Elyda's orders. We'll guide him ourselves."

Daloth hesitated for a moment. Then, with a snort, he nodded. "Of course."

The Monitors addressed the women, "We need the wife's permission."

"Go with them," Zylla told her husband. Kalia stifled a cry.

Zayn followed the Monitors.

*

Expressionless, Zayn entered the High Chamber, obviously unaware of the situation at hand. Elyda waited at the dais. She bade him, "Approach."

He didn't look at her. The Monitors brought Zayn forward. His orange tunic was bright against the green gowns of the Council.

Kaden lowered the hood of his robe, his eyes wide. He walked around Zayn and returned to Cyrll's side.

"Thank you," Elyda nodded. "That's all."

Zayn stared at her.

"You may go." Finally she said, "Take him."

Monitors escorted Zayn out of the High Chamber. Elyda scrutinized Kaden. "Well?"

"During the attack on Yutor I was flung into the shadows, barely conscious. Unable to move or cry out, I watched him slay my friends. I'll never forget his face. That – " Kaden pointed to the space where Zayn had stood " – was the same face."

"How is this possible?"

CHAPTER SEVEN
Choosings

Monitors returned Zayn home. Thayn and Ava sat at the table in the alcove studying for their examinations. Nothing else mattered now. So much was at stake. Answers to the examination questions, almost always, became part of a collection in the library.

On rare occasions, after their Choosings, participants were never seen again. Not because they flunked the examination, Thayn thought to himself, but better to be sure. He sighed.

A huge volume on the history of Eator that he reviewed was a compendium of facts. The names of all its High Ministers. The seasonal volume of bristle produced by every nexus. Winners of the competitions held in the marketplace.

It was horribly incomplete. Thayn knew much of the city and the land that wasn't included. He never questioned how he knew it.

Somehow Ava seemed to understand Thayn's predicament. She suggested in a whisper, "The trick is to keep to what's in this book."

At his loom in an adjacent alcove, Daloth called Zayn. Thayn tilted his head and listened. "Tell me what you saw in the Center," Daloth prompted him.

"Woodswarder." Thayn was surprised that his father managed a response.

Daloth, however, retorted, "We don't speak of Woodswarder here. Go, sit down."

Zayn did as he was told.

Thap foosh went Daloth's loom. He whispered, "Idiot."

Thayn flushed, angry. He wanted to confront Daloth. "Do nothing. Be calm. Daloth is a fool," came the voice in Thayn's head.

Eril, Neela and Zod returned from school. Eril seemed excited, at first, about Thayn and Ava's Choosings. Then she complained that she wasn't feeling well and went to bed. Neela and Zod were sent to invite guests to the party.

*

Thayn and Ava didn't remember having so many neighbors. After sharing a few perfunctory words with them, their guests visited among themselves, feasting on the household's mushrooms, fruit and bread.

More neighbors arrived with their own food and drink. They reminisced, sharing stories from their own youth about their friends and families and their own parties. They – they – *they*. Thayn and Ava barely listened. None of this had anything to do with them.

One of the guests pulled a flute from his tunic pocket and accompanied others who sang. Were they oblivious to everything that Thayn was thinking? His questions, his doubts, his anticipation? Was there much that they didn't share, Thayn wondered, or that they didn't know? The party lasted for hours.

*

Finally, the last guests prepared to leave. Ava had dozed off. Thayn nudged her as they came to offer a last round of obligatory congratulations.

Daloth, as soon as the guests left, said good night. Zylla finished clearing the table. Jiara helped Ava to her room. Kalia smiled as Thayn trudged upstairs.

*

Immediately, it felt to Thayn, morning arrived and, for the last time, he prepared for school. He carefully selected what to wear, brown and yellow. Ava wore pink. They would return home after the examination, dress again, and with their parents proceed to the Hall of Choosing.

All of the candidates met Elyda in the same offices as the previous day. Ava smiled at Rykos as they took their seats, complimenting him. "How nice you look." He wore purple and gray.

The examination consisted of one question to be answered in writing. Elyda asked it aloud, repeating it. "How would you describe the city to one who doesn't know it?"

Thayn glanced at Ava. After mouthing at him, "Be careful," she attended to her own response.

Describe the city? Thayn tried to make a list in his head. Unwanted information came to him. The desert. The body of the land. Kala's righteousness. Images of ancient wars. Deeds of wise men and women. The broken bluffs. The mountains, Kala's mighty shoulders, ribbed highlands and distant hips that together contained the grassy basin through which the great river flowed. Other cities, and around every one of them a Ring of Woodswarder. It was all Forbidden Knowledge.

What did he know about the city based on the teachings at school? Slowly Thayn composed, "Eator is bound by the Wooden Wall... and by love... " He thought for a moment, adding, " …and expectations."

*

The family walked together, Ava, Daloth and Jiara and Thayn, Zayn and Kalia. They all wore green, the color of Eator. They met Rykos and his parents at their nexus' archway and crossed the Great Path, making their way in silence. The time for words had passed.

Along respective inner paths families from every nexus converged upon the Center. Its seamless stone wall opened to admit them. Ministration escorted their anxious company along polished hallways that echoed with their footsteps. They entered a small room unlike any other.

A portion of the Hall of Choosing was uncrafted by hand, a great thrust of living rock. The Center and the city had been built around it.

Elyda stood waiting. She addressed the partici-pants. "The casting of the stones has determined your order." Rykos, who looked a little frightened, would be first. Miara would follow, then Arlos, then Ava – Thayn lost track of Elyda's words, unable to pay at-tention to her, his imagination taking over until – he heard his own name. Thayn would be last.

Rykos hugged his parents and took his place in the middle of the Hall. He faced the Doors of Choosing.

Elyda raised her palm. Framed by fingers of flowing rock, the Doors of Choosing looked similar, but they induced different reactions.

Thayn studied them. They seemed to blink, shifting from side to side. Rykos studied them, too. In a moment that seemed to last forever, the First Door swung wide. Rykos disappeared through it.

Miara took her place. Her turn lasted even longer. Again, the First Door opened.

Arlos was next. The Doors of Choosing blinked. Thayn tried to concentrate, but he blinked, too, and Arlos was gone. Where? "I must follow him," Thayn thought to himself. The world was just beginning to make sense.

He barely noticed Ava take her place. She adjusted her braids. The Second Door opened. Gingerly, Ava stepped through it.

The Doors of Choosing continued to blink. Thayn stared at them, spellbound. One by one, his classmates disappeared, until – "Thayn."

Upon hearing his name, he hugged his father and mother. Kalia smiled. Thayn found strength in it.

He stood for a moment without expression. Kalia looked from father to son and back again. How alike they looked, Thayn knew that she was thinking.

With a nod to Daloth and Jiara, he turned and his eternal instant began. The Doors of Choosing blinked and exchanged positions. The voice in Thayn's head became excited.

Was it Arlos' voice? Thayn felt something that belonged to him – an end without beginning and a beginning without end. Where? Behind which door? He felt a swelling in his soul. The world washed away as the Second Door opened.

"Wait." Something interrupted him. Thayn hesitated on the threshold of maturity, cocking his head. A collective gasp filled the Hall of Choosing as his attention was drawn to the Third Door. A palpable silence followed. "I think – yes – I hear something," he exclaimed.

"What is it?" Elyda's face knitted through several expressions.

"Crying." Something bad was happening behind the Third Door. Somehow Thayn felt responsible for it. "It's the crying of children."

PART TWO

CHAPTER EIGHT
The Third Door

His attention to the Third Door clearly alarmed Thayn's elders. Everyone looked to the High Minister for guidance. Elyda did nothing. She waited patiently until Thayn, not knowing what else to do, stepped through the Second Door and with a shrug disappeared from the Hall of Choosing.

*

Thayn entered the pavilion of the Ring. Its gnarlwood walls were a lattice of light and shadow. He looked up and blinked. The leafy sky above the pavilion was green. It fluttered in the wind, and yellow and blue flickered through it.

Cyrll and his captains were waiting for him. They smiled. Thayn stood naked before them.

Where was Arlos?

"Thayn," hailed Cyrll, "welcome. Your Choosing

honors us."

Everyone stood. Stewards secured around Thayn's waist a woven belt and hung from it white bristlecloth at Thayn's side.

Cyrll approached him. The voice in Thayn's head was quelled by the beating of his heart. He felt Cyrll's thoughts and fell to his knees.

Thayn could sense the High Warden's will. Cyrll offered him a white berry. Thayn extended his tongue and drew the berry between his teeth. He bit down and it squirted. Sweet, it fed a hunger that quickly grew. At the same time came a sense of fulfillment.

He stood and closed his eyes. His temples swelled, it seemed, and as he touched them the sensation grew into his shoulders and reached down the back of his legs, then up again in front until it reached full circle. It intensified along the way. Thayn, too, now, was a Woodsward of legend and exaggeration.

He opened his eyes and looked around in wonder. He ran his hands up and down his sides. He brushed the hair off his brow. Yes, he thought to himself, at least his hair was the same.

Cyrll stepped away. His captains stood to either side of him to form a corridor. Cyrll beckoned and Thayn obeyed him. A Salutation of the Captains introduced Thayn to a new life in the Ring of Eator.

The effect of the white berry was intense, both calming and invigorating. Thayn recognized the first captain to salute him. He was Tylos.

A next captain waited and then another. In time, Thayn stood in front of the High Warden again.

Cyrll's thoughts reached through Thayn's mind like fingers, caressing it. Impossibilities resolved as the same simple answer satisfied countless curiosities and questions. Thayn belonged here. Relieved of all misgivings, Thayn's shoulders quivered and his knees grew weak. He lapsed from consciousness.

With a nod, the captains withdrew. Cyrll carried Thayn to pillows reserved for the occasion. He would rouse again soon.

*

In the chill of dawn an alarm sounded. For a second time Owan's sharp eyes detected a distant figure outside the city. A hastily formed interception party found an old woman in a tattered gray gown, barely alive. She looked at them with rheumy eyes. They brought a bier and carried her into the Ring and then to the Center.

She was a Ministrant of Yutor.

Ministration of Eator nursed her. She clung to a

troubled sleep. At last she opened her eyes wide. "The Third Door – " She slipped away again.

"Yes, my dear?" whispered the Ministrant who attended to her. She stroked the old woman's cheek with her hand.

Her eyes grew wide again. "They came – " her voice trailed off into a whimper " – through the Third Door."

"Call Elyda."

As if in conversation, the old Ministrant of Yutor uttered a string of unintelligible words. With a rattle her head cocked to the side and she was dead.

*

The remnants of a storm accompanied the Ministrant from Yutor. Its lightning was nearly spent, but gusty winds wrung the clouds together until they wept.

The city abbreviated its business. In time even the hardiest workers returned from the fields. The marketplace and smithies stood empty. Children stayed inside at school and their parents enjoyed an unusual day at home together. No one, except Axl, witnessed several Woodswarder disguised as Monitors bring the old Ministrant to the Center, and no rumors spread.

*

After his welcome, Thayn was removed to a snug

96

bower adjacent to the High Camp. Leafy vines woven among slender trees formed walls and a high ceiling. Thayn slept on a low wooden platform. He rolled onto his back and stretched out his arms, upsetting several pillows. He returned an arm to brush his brow, leaving the other arm dangling at his side.

He blinked several times. His lips twitched, then relaxed into a smile. His eyes fluttered and closed again. The bower was still. The light was soft. High overhead the canopy did its best to deflect the storm. Nevertheless, rainwater misted and dripped.

The pillows were retrieved and tucked back around him. His arm was gently lifted and replaced, his hand coming to rest along his abdomen. An old man sat by his side.

*

Retired to her modest stone chamber deep within the Center, Jovia slept fitfully. She flailed her arms, then pulled them to her breast, twisting her bedclothes. As she fought to release herself, one hand emerged and she shook it in the air.

Her young and ungainly nurse, Halla, calmed her and straightened her bedclothes. "There, there." She smoothed the old woman's hair. Jovia was dreaming.

*

In her dream, two young faces appeared in front of Jovia. One was soft in its expression. The other hardened. The first face belonged to a boy who fell to the ground. The second belonged to a boy who pushed him. Twins.

Years later, as young men, the twins stood in front of the Doors of Choosing. The first twin took his place and the Second Door opened. The second twin joined him at the threshold, not waiting his turn. The first twin backed away from his brother and a battle of wills ensued. The First Door opened, too.

Jovia interceded, stepping between the twins. The first twin escaped through the First Door. The second twin objected, regarding the High Minister with an expression of malevolence. He raised an arm against her. Jovia opened her palm. The second twin skidded backwards as the Third Door swung wide. "No." He stumbled through it and it slammed shut.

*

A tunnel led the second twin to a forsaken wasteland. He escaped it and explored the mountains and grasslands of Kala. In time he located what – whom – he sought.

The first twin lived a quiet life in Eator after returning through the First Door. He married, worked in the fields and began a family. A new face appeared, a baby boy who looked like his father.

The second twin attempted to enter the woods that surrounded the city. Without warning a sudden force slapped him away, returning him to the wasteland. He cursed Kala.

Learning at the expense of whomever he met, the second twin wandered the land. Disfigured by his own cruelty, he was shunned by Outcasts. He located other cities and attempted to enter them. Again forces repelled him to the wasteland. "Alak," he lamented.

Resolving to avoid the cities, he followed the great river to its source and discovered caverns of pink and white. He found inscribed tablets and a bush of berries. From them he acquired new powers.

He returned to Eator and, from a safe distance outside its defenses, enjoined his brother in thought.

*

As a schoolboy, the son of the first twin watched his father sit surrounded by Forbidden Books. His face was animated. Jovia entered their dwelling. No longer himself, the first twin and Jovia argued. She saw in him a malevolence that she had witnessed only once.

Their eyes locked. He raised his hand to her. She opened her palm. Before she had time to do anything more, something horrible happened. He slumped over. She roused him, but his face was expressionless. His mind was closed. "I didn't do this," Jovia protested to the Monitors.

*

Years later, attending to business of the city, Jovia visited the Forbidden Room. Books were open. Pages turned by themselves. She screamed and all the books snapped shut. She remembered a young man – once a boy – and hurried out through the alcove to the table where he sat just moments ago. The chair was empty, but this time she remembered who he was.

*

Her dream concluded, Jovia smiled in her sleep as Elyda entered the chamber. "Thank you, Halla. I'll sit with her."

"Have you eaten?" Halla asked.

"I'm not hungry," Elyda replied. She looked older, if that were possible, and even more careworn.

Halla pursed her lips.

"Go." She obeyed.

Elyda reflected on Jovia's distress. There had been subtle changes in her distemper, interludes of something that Elyda didn't understand, but no signs of improvement.

Oilstem sent flickers of light and shadow across Jovia's face. Again dreaming, her lips moved quickly now. She was speaking, arguing until frustration swept over her and she flailed her arms again.

Jovia's chamber felt stark and barren. Elyda knew the room well and had never regarded it so. It had always been a source of energy, a well-spring of determination and authority. These were qualities of its occupant, however, not of the room.

The walls offered her no welcome. Jovia was the symbol of stability that the city held sacred. She, mere Elyda, couldn't live up to such expectations. The cold stone reviled her, she could feel it. She sat beside her troubled charge and wandered through her own dark thoughts.

Elyda was exhausted. She had been in meetings the better part of the morning. The Ministrant of Yutor had been brought to her, dead. Her news was repeated. In response, with the approval of the High Council, Elyda sealed the Third Door.

*

Thayn stirred again. He blinked his eyes and almost sat up, resting back on his elbows. He looked blankly around the leafy bower and at the old man who sat by his side. His severe features were dominated by a beaky nose. "Hello."

"Hello," the old man squeaked.

"Where am I?"

"Home." Thayn stood up and stretched, working a kink out of his lower back. Mulch crunched underfoot. He walked to a wall stacked with basketry and, peering through the vines, observed the High Camp. The pavilion stood in the middle of its great clearing. Thayn heard the wind wail and water dripping. The old man inquired in a shrill voice, "Are you rested?"

Thayn turned. "Yes, thank you." His inquisitive expression was insincere. For reasons that he didn't understand, Thayn didn't like the old man.

The old man seemed to sense Thayn's misgivings. He pursed his lips as if about to laugh, but coughed instead. He bent over, sputtering and wheezing. After a moment he straightened himself, looked at Thayn and cleared his throat. "I'm Lor." His eyes were piercing.

"I'm Thayn."

"I'm aware of that," Lor squeaked. "There's much you have to learn, young man. I'm here to attend to you until you're no longer in need of me."

Thayn walked to the doorway of the bower. The view outside was thick with saplings and ferns. A narrow pathway reached through them.

A gust of wind slammed against the canopy high overhead. It was followed by a lick of rain. Thayn had little idea where he was and absolutely no sense of purpose. Nevertheless, he didn't feel in need of anyone – except Arlos – and some answers.

Where was he? What happened to everybody else? Where *was* Arlos? Thayn wanted to look for him – to leave this place. Could he?

The wind whimpered. Thayn looked up as a fat raindrop splattered against his brow. "Oh." Memories of the previous night flooded over him and slowly soaked away.

"You have many things to do," interrupted Lor's shrill voice. "One of them will earn you this."

Thayn turned.

Lor held up the green bristlecloth that hung from his belt. "Until then, I'll teach you."

Thayn didn't think that he wanted to be taught – certainly not by this old dut. He looked out the doorway of the bower and along the path again.

"To begin, you'll explore the Ring. You'll greet every Woodsward. Let me show you how." Lor approached him and knelt. "It's your First Task."

Thayn's eyes grew wide. He looked down at the old man. He wanted to get away, but he didn't know where to go. He was afraid to ask questions – the old man reminded him of Daloth and he didn't want to get in trouble.

He took a few steps backwards, conflicted. Again the old man seemed to know Thayn's mind. "You may begin."

"What?"

"Go," Lor shrieked. "Go."

"Oh." Thayn ran out of the bower and into the Ring. Lor laughed and coughed.

*

Jovia sighed and opened her eyes. Elyda sat asleep in her chair. "Are you all right, my child?" she called to her.

Elyda roused. "Praise Kala." She knelt at Jovia's side, hugging her.

"I've been away?" Jovia asked.

Elyda nodded. "Where?"

Jovia sighed. "I'm not sure. But I'm back – and I'm hungry."

Elyda brought them food and they shared a simple meal together. Then Elyda helped Jovia freshen herself. She attended to her quickly, worried that her lucidity wouldn't last.

Finally they sat together and visited as Elyda remembered their visits to be. The room became vibrant again. Elyda shared with Jovia events as they had unfolded since her collapse.

*

Kaden was immediately summoned to the Center. This time he came alone. The rain continued and he arrived drenched.

After exchanging his wet robe for a dry one Kaden was guided, not to the High Chamber, but to Jovia's bedside. She questioned him more thoroughly. His face was grim in the flickering oilstem as he recounted in detail the attack on Yutor. Asked to describe his adversary, Kaden described a face that Jovia knew.

"And – " He hesitated.

"Tell me," she encouraged him.

"It's nothing."

"Perhaps not."

"'Alak' he said. Over and over. 'Alak.'"

Jovia tilted her head. Then she looked at him hard, her deep blue eyes meeting his. "Tell me, what do you know of the Third Door?"

"The Third Door? It's part of Choosings. It's for the unloving, isn't it?"

"You know nothing more about it?"

Kaden shook his head.

"A Ministrant from your city arrived this morning," Jovia continued. "She's dead. I'm sorry. She corroborates your report. The attack on your city came from within. Through the Third Door."

"How is this possible?" Kaden asked.

"A frequent question lately." Jovia smiled sadly. "As you have no doubt heard, at present I'm beset with bouts of madness. As a result, I'm unable to separate my dreams from reality, my facts from my fears. Until that is possible, I hesitate to offer you an answer to your question."

"I see." Kaden appreciated her honesty.

"I wish I had words that would make things better, but I don't," Jovia admitted, "so I'll say nothing more. But know that our thanks and warm welcome continue. You may go."

*

Thayn hurried along a path that led away from the bower through a thicket of saplings overgrown with ferns. The path turned several times before reaching the High Camp. He looked across it. The clearing was spongy with moss and misty with rain. The pavilion glistened. High above branches formed intersecting arches that fluttered in the wind.

Thayn examined the leafy perimeter of the High

Camp. Nowhere along its wall could he detect a trace of Lor's bower.

He oriented himself. Thayn was anxious to get away, but he knew that he was expected to return. He didn't want to become lost. A distinctive tree with shaggy bark would serve him as a marker.

He skirted the High Camp, making his way to the nearer end. What, he wondered, bothered him about the old man? He didn't know. He'd think about it some other time. A number of paths led through the understory. Thayn chose one of them and followed it.

It led him to the Wooden Wall. He had only seen it from the fields on the other side and never so close. Mighty tree trunks appeared to have oozed together as if laced and pulled tight.

Thayn passed no one along the way. He found a wash station and, after a brief visit, felt much better. A new choice of paths was waiting. He began to explore the Ring. It possessed a pristine beauty, especially in the rain, soft moss underfoot and ferns everywhere. Bushes of bright red berries sprawled among eager saplings that prepared to join the senior trees in support of the fluttering green-golden canopy.

Thayn noticed small clearings within the passing thickets. In several of them Woodswarder fraternized, engaging in social activities that were new to him, although most of the Woodwarder waited out the storm. Curious but shy, Thayn continued on his way.

Above the canopy the gusty wind whipped away at the withering billows. Thicker swells rode in on their backs and settled over Eator resulting in a gentler, but steady, rain.

An old tree grew not far from the path. Long ago it had lost its trunk. Branches that forked low to the ground took its place. They slanted away from one another to serve as seating around the old stump. Three young men sat within the tree talking softly and laughing. One of them looked at Thayn as he approached. Their eyes met.

"Come. Join us," he called. He sounded friendly enough. As Thayn stepped into the tree he added with a smile, "You're on your First Task?"

"He notices my white bristlecloth," Thayn thought to himself and replied aloud, "Yes."

"This is Jaric and Waryn." Both of them wore their hair in braids. Smiling, he added, "I'm Jad."

"I'm Thayn."

"When did you arrive?"

"Yesterday – I think. I've been asleep."

They smiled. "We remember you from school."

Several years older than Thayn, they were all from a different nexus.

"Of course." Thayn hesitated. "Do you remember Arlos, too?"

"From Nexus Five?"

"I do."

"He isn't here."

"He isn't? But – " Thayn was confused, both disappointed and –

"Aren't you going to greet us?"

"Oh, my First Task." As Lor demonstrated, Thayn greeted Jaric, Waryn and Jad. He was too enthusiastic.

"Careful."

Thayn flushed, embarrassed. "I need to go." He hurried out of the tree.

"Wait," Jad called after him. He followed Thayn along the path. "Where do you need to go?"

Thayn stopped. He didn't really know. "Around the Ring," he replied at last.

"It's a long way." Jad walked past Thayn backwards, glancing at his companions. Again, Jaric and Waryn smiled. "And it's raining."

"I don't mind."

"There are paths that twist and turn, both here and above." Jad looked up into the canopy. "Perhaps I'll accompany you, at least part of the way."

They walked along the path until Jad sprang up into the trees. Thayn followed. Other Woodswarder perched in them. They were thick and limber and the view was exhilarating. Thayn had never climbed so high.

Jad and Thayn reached the network of branches and bridging that extended throughout the canopy. Smaller branches above them swayed in the storm and rain dripped through the leaves, but beneath them their feet stayed sure.

Traveling through the treetops, they progressed through several sectors of the Ring. Jad showed Thayn how to spot features that weren't obvious to the eye, the gates, the towers and other posts. He pointed out some of the clearings below them and described their activities. In a few of them, berry bushes grew in cultivated patches.

Between descriptions Jad sang softly to himself as they traveled through the trees. He wanted to check with friends in an upcoming clearing that, in no time, opened below them. A sweet smell reached up through the mist. Jad invited Thayn to join him. "You would be popular among the carvers."

Jad looked at him with an expression that made

Thayn feel several ways at the same time. His heart pounded in his ears, and he felt a little self-conscious, but he didn't feel awkward anymore. Nevertheless, the voice in his head dissuaded him. "No – but thanks." He turned to go.

Jad reached after him. He pulled Thayn to him, put his hand behind Thayn's neck and kissed him. "Find me here – whenever you're ready." Jad slipped down the tree.

Thayn stared after him. He still felt pressure at the back of his head. He touched his hand to his lips and blinked his eyes. No berry or thought of Arlos prepared Thayn for the feelings that flooded him now. As they receded, preconceptions and misconceptions were swept away. Thayn almost descended after Jad, but a surge of vulnerability overwhelmed him. He hurried away through the trees.

*

Jad dropped into the clearing. It was carpeted with moss and edged with feathery ferns. He waved at friends. Kaden had just returned from Jovia's chamber and sat beside Owan relating his news.

CHAPTER NINE
Breaking of arms

Thayn continued his exploration of the Ring. Or was it all a dream? Again he touched his lips – lips that had just been kissed – and with his other hand he rubbed the back of his neck. "Oh." He almost slipped. Routes through the treetops branched this way and that and grew much too narrow for him to navigate easily. He decided that the footpaths would be safer and climbed down from the trees.

There were a few distractions along the way. He greeted passing Woodswarder. "Thayn?" He heard a familiar voice, one that he no longer expected to hear.

"Arlos?" As he had in the marketplace and school-yard garden, Arlos stood in front of Thayn, this time unencumbered by anything that might disguise his true feelings. Thayn asked him, "Arlos, it that really you? I thought – "

"Come with me," Arlos encouraged Thayn.

"Where?"

"This way." Thayn followed Arlos to the edge of the Ring.

"Where are you going?"

"We – *we* are going." They stepped into the tall grass. Sodden from the storm, the grasslands stretched as far as the eye could see.

Caution seized Thayn. "No."

"Come." Arlos' will was undeniable, but Thayn experienced an even stronger urge to refuse him. At last Arlos snarled, "Why do you suppose you've come this far, you fool?"

Arlos would never say that to him. Thayn backed away, whispering, "Who are you?"

As if in reply, Arlos' familiar face and lithe body twitched and flinched, returning to that of their owner, a stocky Woodsward who looked about himself in absolute confusion.

Thayn ran. He didn't stop until the pavilion reappeared before him. He skirted the High Camp, this time from the opposite direction, until he found the tree with shaggy bark that marked the path to Lor's bower. He sat against it and caught his breath.

*

Again Monitors visited Thayn's household. This time Zayn was escorted, not to the High Chamber, but to Jovia's bedside.

"Elyda, go."

"Leave you alone with him?" Zayn, handsome in purple, stood motionless. His face wore no expression.

"Yes."

With a sigh of frustration, Elyda left.

*

"Let me look at you." Jovia slipped to the floor and walked around Zayn several times. "Never ignore a problem hoping it will go away. Your brother remains, without a doubt, the bane of my existence."

When Jovia attempted to contact the High Minister of Yutor, she discovered in her place an unexpected intruder. She was no match for the evil that he had become. "You, Zayn, are blameless, of course. It's taken me too long to appreciate your selflessness. I never questioned why you were such a good boy."

Again reaching out in thought, Jovia visited Zayn's mind, something that she hadn't attempted since the night of his so-called accident many years ago. "Oh." She found almost nothing there.

Under normal circumstances, Jovia would have abandoned her task, but her very madness emboldened her. "I've come to conclude your good nature is accidental, which makes you all the more blameless. Your son shares your disposition, by the way, tempered by his mother's sensibility which has some mischief to it." She smiled. Then, with intense concentration, she whispered quick words.

Over a considerable interval of time, Zayn's eyes acquired focus and he took on an inquisitive expression. He returned Jovia's smile.

She waited patiently. "Can you hear me?"

"I look through a window where once there was no wall," Zayn explained, "but I'm here."

"I didn't do this to you. Years ago when I discovered you had taken books from the Forbidden Room, I attempted to erase your memory of them. I entered your thoughts. They were so troubled, so painful, that I withdrew. You slumped over. Your mind was closed – violently – but not by me." Jovia had considered the incident her greatest failing, never understanding what had happened until the onset of her madness.

"It was Vok," Zayn informed her.

"It's as I fear." She asked, "Where is he now?"

"I'm not sure. He must be distracted."

"'Alak – ?'"

Zayn interrupted her with a laugh. "Does he still

115

say that?"

"What does it mean?"

"Backwards it – " Flinching, Zayn stopped short. With effort he charged her, "Take care – of my – son."

"Zayn?"

His face screwed up, then slackened again. Jovia heard a voice in her head whisper, "Foolish woman," and felt a lick of pain.

"Oh," she cried and fell back in bed.

*

Elyda rushed into the room to find Jovia unconscious. Zayn stood as he had when she left them, expressionless. She called Monitors to return him home.

*

Thayn returned to Lor's bower, thinking about Jad and Arlos. He tried to separate what was real from what he was sure that he imagined.

"Good, you've returned," Lor shrieked. Thayn felt him touch his mind, but the old man recoiled. "Oh, the disorganization. I'm too old for such things.

"So tell me in your own words," he continued, "everything you've learned about the Ring, and then I'll tell you more."

Thayn decided not to share too freely. He described the watch posts and patches of berries.

"You'll spend time in them soon," Lor squeaked. "And stocking the stations. Your duties, after you complete your First Task, will be various. You'll see."

"What do I need to do?"

"You'll see, I said. You'll guard us with your eyes and attend to our well-being. Of greatest importance is care of the berries. Every leaf must be checked every day. All must be free of disease. Its trace is ephemeral. If the bush isn't destroyed immediately, blight will spread and all will be lost."

"I've seen berry bushes growing everywhere."

"Red berries. Don't eat them. The others require cultivation. They have greater powers. Now tell me about the clearings," Lor continued.

"I saw some of them and he showed me – "

"He?" Conflicting expressions played across Lor's thin face.

"But I didn't go – "

"Good," Lor interrupted. "You've no business in them until you've completed your lessons."

Lor sat at one end of the platform. He reached to retrieve a basket. "These are for you. From Cyrll."

"What are they?" Thayn asked.

"You may examine them." They were of various sizes, representations of Kala carved from roots of trees. "And this."

Lor held between his thumb and forefinger a pink berry. "This will expand your potential. Tell me as we work everything you know about Kala, and then I'll tell you more."

"More? Kala is everything and all. From many he made one and from one he made many."

"Your berry."

Thayn swallowed it. Its effect was immediate.

"You know what you've been taught in school," Lor observed, reaching for a bowl of greenfruit. The lesson began. "Kala fell out of Before Time and into the desert to become the body of the land. All was at peace while the Ancient Days were young. Unknown to Kala, however, with him came unwanted guests and unwanted thoughts. His people grew proud and intolerant of one another and their hatred bred fear. Villages fought and fell. The wise among them fled. The remaining inhabitants were seduced by parasites of the land.

"No matter into what configurations the Ancient Days slipped, the cycles of intolerance, hatred, fear and pride continued among communities of Kala, between neighbors in the streets and within families around the hearth.

"The wise were attracted to an abrupt thrust of rock within a scattering of trees. Growing from a cleft in its side was a bush of colored berries. The berries offered strength and great wisdom. From throughout the land the enlightened found the little community. It grew in secrecy.

"The berries expanded their perception. In silent communication the wise discovered stray thoughts of Kala that had escaped Before Time. Utilizing these thoughts they designed and crafted the first of today's cities. The Doors of Choosing were recognized and the stones were carved. Into them was placed power that anticipated, and made manifest, harmony and balance. It was the will of Kala.

"Meanwhile, war overcame the Ancient Days. Everything lay in ruin. The land shuddered, gouged and split. A party of the wise claimed those left of the living for whom there was still promise. A next city was organized. Once established, from it another party set out and over time the present cities were founded. The Ancient Days drew to a close.

"The stones determine the time of birth and death and Choosing. According to their love, men and women who pass through the First Door find themselves in the temple of the Genexus. Those who pass through the Second Door find themselves in the pavilion of the Woodswarder or in the High Chamber. The Third Door is reserved for those who don't love."

Lor concluded his lesson by listing the cities of Kala. Thayn reviewed them in his head. He looked up at the old man. "You forgot Evator,"

He seemed, at first, simply irritated by the correction. Then, after thinking for a moment, Lor grew confounded. He coughed. "You already know of the other cities?" he squeaked.

Thayn nodded.

"But this is Forbidden Knowledge."

*

Night stretched across Eator and the storm abated. The Ministrant from Yutor was laid to rest. Her funeral pyre burnt bright as a pale moon rose in the sky.

Jovia slept and, again, she dreamt.

*

In her dream Kaden stared from the shadows at someone whom she recognized as Vok.

He stepped into flickering light, but he wasn't Vok. Was he – Zayn?

Kaden lunged at him with a knife to his throat. He wasn't Zayn, either. Was he – Thayn?

*

Jovia sat up and screamed. Halla attempted to comfort her. Jovia whispered, "Find Elyda. Communicate with Cyrll. Tell him what I have to say."

*

Thayn awoke and rubbed his eyes. He had fallen asleep after his lesson. Lor dozed now, snoring softly. Thayn nibbled at fruit and hardloaf that the old man set out for him.

He decided to venture again into the Ring, traveling through the trees. Woodswarder hailed Thayn and he greeted them in return.

In time he found the clearing that Jad had joined the previous day. A Woodward who perched in a tree appeared to him, momentarily, as Arlos. He appealed, "Come with me – "

Ignoring him, Thayn dropped to the mossy floor.

" – or you'll be sorry," the Woodsward called after him in the same voice that Thayn heard in his head.

Carvers sat around fires rekindled after the rain. From pliant roots they fashioned depictions of Kala and members of the Woodswarder.

Thayn heard his name and turned. A figure passed in and out of the light. "I'm glad you're here."

"Jad?"

He embraced Thayn. "This way." Thayn followed

121

Jad through feathery ferns to a flickering fire. Around it sat Woodswarder whom Thayn recognized. Kaden and Owan chopped herbs for salve.

Thayn stepped out of the shadow. Kaden looked up in disbelief. He saw – was he – Vok?

Kaden sprang to his feet, holding his knife in front of him, frozen. Thayn and Jad took a step backwards. Owan scrambled next to Kaden. "What are you – ?"

Guards rushed into the clearing. Cyrll sent them, but it was too late.

*

A guard later described to Cyrll the strange alter-cation that followed. It required some sorting out. As Kaden lunged at Thayn with the knife, Jad and Owan reacted simultaneously.

The knife flashed toward Thayn. Jad deflected Kaden's forearm with his own. *Crack.* Kaden's arm broke. The knifepoint grazed Thayn's throat.

Owan extended his arm, himself intending to de-flect the knife. Instead his arm slammed against Jad's. *Crack.* Jad's arm broke.

Thayn reacted, too. His arm met Owan's. *Crack.* Owan's arm broke.

Kaden, Jad and Owan clutched their broken arms. Thayn held a hand to his throat. They stared at one another.

*

Thayn was returned to the bower that he shared with Lor and the old man tended to his wound. The other Woodswarder were taken to the High Camp. A steward set their broken bones, fashioning slings from vine and binding their arms.

*

Again, Jovia's chamber filled.

CHAPTER TEN
Many partings

Cyrll accompanied Kaden and Thayn to Jovia's chamber. Monitors escorted Zayn. This time, Elyda remained.

Zayn had yet to dress for the day. Both in robes, the similarity between father and son was pronounced. Neither was the man whom Kaden remembered, but both of them so closely resembled him, and each other.

Kaden circled them in confusion.

"We don't have much time," Jovia interrupted. "I'm strong for the moment, but it won't last long."

It took some explanation for Thayn fully to understand all that had been happening. He knew little of his father's brother. Jovia told them, "An excellent student, he was deeply, deeply troubled. He's acquired great strength. Strength about which we no longer teach. I must remember it myself as I go along. Or

I consult books in the Forbidden Room."

She looked at Thayn. He averted his eyes.

"I spoke to your father earlier, Thayn."

He looked back at her.

"Not as he is now, but as he was before his mind was closed. I didn't do that to him, you know. You witnessed it, didn't you, standing in the shadow? I've never spoken of it to you. It was Vok who closed his mind."

"Vok?" Cyrll whispered.

"Oh," Elyda cried.

"It's Vok I fight." Jovia held her fingertips to the side of her head. Thayn did the same. "Your father's a brave man, Thayn. As are you. His last words today charged me with your protection."

She addressed Kaden. "It's Vok who has taken your city. He's the twin of Zayn and uncle of this young man whose throat you tried to cut. Kala warned me in a dream. I was almost too late."

Kaden's expression changed from wonder to rue.

"When," Jovia asked Thayn, "did you first hear your uncle's voice?"

It was on the way to school after his father's so-called accident. That morning Arlos looked different to him. So many things became clear to Thayn now.

The voice in his head offering guidance and praise – and persuasion – had never been his father's voice – or Arlos'. It was his uncle's. Why?

And what had Thayn done to make this Woodsward, Kaden, hate him so?

Another thought came to him. He asked, "Vok went through the Third Door?"

"Yes."

"And it was children I heard," he added, unsure of what his observation meant.

The others looked at him. Thayn's involvement in recent events had almost been forgotten. Elyda related details of Thayn's Choosing.

"Children?" Kaden wondered aloud.

"No," Jovia screamed, "he's upon me again." Immediately her hands were on her head. Her eyes grew wide. She fell back onto her bed and lapsed into unconsciousness.

"You need to leave now," Elyda told them. She went to the door and called, "Halla."

Halla met them in the outer passage.

"Sit with Jovia," Elyda instructed. "I must check on our other patient. Where is Arlos?"

"I – "

"Arlos?" Thayn interrupted. "Did you say Arlos?"

" – moved him in there." Halla pointed across the hall.

"What happened to him?" Thayn asked, his heart pounding involuntarily. "May I see him?"

Elyda shook her head in annoyance. "Absolutely not. No visitors."

*

Reluctantly, Thayn returned to the Ring. Father. Arlos. Vok. He needed to rethink everything, but he wanted only to block it from his mind.

His First Task would distract him from his troubled thoughts. Many Woodswarder lived among the trees. Thayn greeted them. None appeared to Thayn now as anyone other than himself.

*

Thayn didn't return to Lor's bower until morning. Lor tended to his throat, replacing the dressing. Thayn said to him, "You're a Woodsward of the Ring."

"Yes," Lor squeaked, "what of it?"

"I must have greeted everybody by now." Thayn looked at Lor for a moment. So thin and severe, he was almost comical. "I haven't greeted you, have I?"

An odd expression flashed across Lor's face. It passed quickly. "As you wish."

Thayn knelt. "There." Exhausted, he slept most of

the day.

*

That evening Thayn felt a presence. Or was he dreaming? No – he felt it again. It was inside his head, a new voice. Jovia called to Thayn. She told him to come to her, quietly.

Careful not to disturb Lor, who had nodded off after their lesson, Thayn hurried through the trees to the Wooden Wall. He grabbed a robe from one of the wash stations and slipped through the next sector gate.

Why, Thayn wondered, didn't the guards call after him? He hurried along an empty outer path. Crossing the Great Path he saw only a few Genexus who, thinking that he was a Monitor, ignored him.

Jovia directed Thayn to the library. He entered unseen through a side door and made his way in the dark through a maze of tables. They met in the musty Forbidden Room. Oilstem flickered against the wall.

"Why am I here?" Thayn asked.

"Your friend Arlos. He's dead."

"What?" Jovia continued, but Thayn barely heard her. His eyes brimmed with tears as she described Arlos' brief struggle.

"Why did it happen?" she asked. "We don't know. You *do*, don't you? Is it the work of Vok? Have you done something to anger him?"

Jovia's question returned Thayn to the moment. "How do you know? You weren't there."

"What did you do?"

"Arlos – appeared – in the Ring. He wanted me to follow him into the grasslands."

"You resisted him – how? Why?"

"I don't know. I sensed something wasn't – real."

"Too good to be true – ? As your father is – ? As you are – ? No. Your sense of rightness is a trait you share with your mother. It has protected you.

"May Kala protect us all. Your uncle, Thayn, has become quite a problem. Something must be done."

Thayn and Jovia visited long into the night. She spoke of duty. She taught him incantations from the Forbidden Books. They held their palms together.

*

Hours later Thayn returned to an empty bower. On the low platform lay a green bristlecloth. Where was Lor?

*

Jovia returned to her modest stone chamber and crawled into bed. To her surprise, the wall at the foot of her bed melted and a doorway opened. "Oh." A young Ministrant with a long red braid froze when she saw Jovia. She wore a white gown.

"What are you doing, child?"

"I'm sorry. Please, excuse me. I'm still learning my way."

"By holding your palm to walls?" Jovia studied her. "Perhaps it would be better to wait until you've been taught."

Ava flushed, but returned the old woman's stare. "I'm in a hurry."

Jovia arched her brow, narrowed her eyes and patted the bed beside her. "Come sit by me."

*

News spread throughout the city the following morning. Arlos, Lor, Jovia, and Boz, the baker, had passed away during the night. Arrangements would be made for four funerals. Ashes would be scattered in the Fallow Field.

*

Earlier that morning Thayn wondered what Lor would ask him about his absence and how he would keep Jovia's secrets. Instead, he discovered that Lor was gone.

Where? Lor was never away. And why would he leave his bristlecloth? Carefully folded, it lay next to Thayn's pillow.

It was too late to sleep. His mind racing, Thayn decided to go back out into the Ring and continue his First Task. That would divert him.

Thayn heard a faint rustle outside the bower. Lor? No, it was too far away.

The rustle grew into a roar. A furious whoosh of wind rushed in, ripping the bower walls. The ceiling split. Thayn turned as the wind whirled around him. Leaves slapped against him as they spiraled into the branches overhead. Lor's bristlecloth was carried along with them, billowing white. Violently, the trees rocked back and forth.

As quickly as it came, the wind was gone. Silence settled over the broken bower. Thayn looked around him. Branches lay scattered everywhere. How could this happen? Poor Lor, this was his home.

Thayn noticed that the bristlecloth that hung at his side was green. How did *that* happen? Could it have been the wind?

His head hurt. Thayn held a hand to it. It was too full. Too many answers, too many questions. Where was Lor?

"Here I am," a voice called to Thayn.

He didn't trust it. Thayn walked through a wall that was no longer there and into the High Camp. He needed to escape this place – and his thoughts. He stepped over broken bits of basketry and woven vine.

He needed to go somewhere, anywhere.

*

By night a gray glimmer bathed the Ring. The high vaults and clearings never succumbed to darkness. Or had Thayn's eyes grown stronger?

He ascended into the trees and traveled into the next sector, passing several Woodswarder. None of them hailed Thayn this night. It was his green bristlecloth, he realized.

Thayn decided to visit a clearing.

Clearings were frequented according to activity by Woodswarder of shared interest. A few were unspecific in their use, offering general recreation. Thayn found one of these. Men visited together, quietly entertaining themselves. Thayn joined several Woodswarder whom he didn't recognize.

"We've yet to meet you, my friend," observed one of them.

"Yet your bristlecloth is green," remarked another.

"I thought I'd greeted everybody by now," Thayn admitted, "but I guess not."

"You may still greet us if you like."

"Wait." The Woodswarder plucked red berries

from a nearby bush. "You were told not to eat these, weren't you?"

"Yes."

"They're yours now. They offer no great power or wisdom, but you'll like the way they make you feel."

Thayn crushed a berry between his teeth. It was tart, then sweet. He looked at the Woodswarder.

They ate them, too. Their eyes sparkled. "So, tell us about yourself."

At last, Thayn was welcomed as a peer.

*

If he slept at all, Thayn didn't know. It was day. He lay among the ferns at the side of the clearing. The effect of the berries slowly subsided.

He stood and stretched. His unsteady legs became stable again. What time was it? Thayn sensed, for some reason, that it didn't matter.

As he stepped through the shadows he found himself already at the edge of a next clearing. He decided that he wouldn't visit it now. Thayn made for a wash station along the Wooden Wall.

As he walked under the adjacent sector gate, news of Lor reached him. The guards spoke of it. "Lor, the Great One?"

"That's what I heard," replied a low voice.

Thayn paused to listen.

"I didn't know he was still alive," came a higher voice. "I thought he lived only in our honor."

"It's been ages since he was High Warden."

"He was very old."

Thayn held to a tree trunk. High Warden? And had the guard said "was"? Their conversation continued, but Thayn barely heard them.

"You knew him?" asked the higher voice.

"When I first arrived. He hasn't been seen in a long time."

"I heard he refused to attend his last tribute."

"Or leave his bower. Now he's with Kala and at peace," concluded the low voice.

"No," Thayn whispered. He pulled himself to his feet and hurried away. He must go to Lor. Thayn hadn't gone far when he overheard another group of Woodswarder.

"Jovia?"

"That's what I heard."

"Tell me it isn't so."

"Dead?" came another voice.

"It was just announced by our captain."

They continued to speak, but Thayn was gone. He ran to the High Camp and aimed toward the tree with shaggy bark that marked the path to – ?

To where? Thayn stopped. Why was he running? Lor was dead, wasn't he?

He returned to the broken bower. Thayn had no reason to go there, but he had no reason to go anywhere else. His head ached. He wanted to cry. He wanted – he didn't know what he wanted.

He didn't expect to find Cyrll piecing through the rubble. He looked older, spent. "Lor has been removed to the pavilion."

On the platform rested a pile of Lor's possessions. Cyrll pulled a white bristlecloth out from under a branch. A strong expression flickered across his face, an expression that Thayn didn't recognize. It scared Thayn and he took a step backwards. "I didn't – I don't understand," he tried to explain.

"It doesn't matter." Cyrll placed the bristlecloth on the platform and sat down. Had he no other place to go, either?

Thayn saw something in Cyrll that he had seen in Lor, something that he hadn't understood until now. It was the loneliness of power. A contradiction.

He knew what he needed to do, although it frightened him. He sat next to the High Warden. Cyrll lay his head in Thayn's lap, sobbing. His tears were wet

135

and hot. Thayn ran his fingers across the great man's temple.

After a few minutes, Cyrll stood. He picked from the pile a short knife, walked to a broken wall and cut away at it. Thayn picked up another knife and joined him. Soon no trace of the bower remained.

The morning grew no brighter. Unhappy clouds filled the sky over Eator.

*

The oilstem in the chamber pulsed with licks of flame. Shadows shifted. Ava sat with Jovia only for a short time but, more than once before they parted, time stood still within itself.

They exchanged few words. Instead, Ava heard Jovia in her thinking and the questions that she wanted to ask were answered all at once. "The incantations I'm about to share with you will make no sense, for the time being, at least. Let us pray they never do," came the thoughts of the old woman.

Ava shared Jovia's palm.

"I'll tell you more later. Now you must go." The old woman spoke aloud, "Go. Elyda's coming."

Ava blinked. "Oh." She roused herself and returned to the wall.

"Hurry." Ava placed her palm to it. A doorway

melted open and she rushed through it. "Hurry."

As the door shut, a puff of air squeezed past. It followed Ava down the hall and swirled around her. Ava threw out her arms to steady herself, closing her eyes.

Her gown fluttered and pulled all about her. Her hair fell out of its braid. As quickly as it came, the puff was gone. Everything was still.

Ava smoothed her gown and, as she ran quietly to her room, she twisted her hair together. It was almost morning, but all she wanted to do was sleep.

The room was dark. She didn't notice that her gown was green.

*

Jovia lied. Elyda came hours later and found Jovia dead, a white gown at her feet. Elyda's sadness was complete. It was sadness for Jovia's passing, sadness for the city, sadness for herself. She felt her existence grow dry and brittle.

The doorway at the foot of Jovia's bed opened. Ava stood in it. Naked, she held the green gown in front of her. She looked at Jovia and Elyda.

"I don't want this," Ava said. "I didn't take it."

"You did – you took her place." Elyda held her fist to her mouth and looked at Ava through swollen

137

eyes. Then she softened. "It can't be otherwise."

"I – I want to go home."

"You *are* home." The two women looked at each other. Ava's chin quivered.

She ran into Elyda's arms. They wept together.

*

The marketplace prepared for business as usual early that morning, all except Boz's booth. The sky grew white. "Where are they?" Rykos wondered. He and Aryla had yet to marry, but Rykos started every day here before joining his parents in the fields.

Rykos hurried to Boz' house. The door blew open as he arrived and a blast of warm air greeted him. An eddy of smoke danced around his head and left a streak of gray in his hair.

He entered. "Aryla?" She stood at the sink with her back to him, washing dishes. Burnt pastries sat on the counter.

Boz sat slumped against the wall next to several ovens in a large, well-organized kitchen. His eyes didn't blink. "He's too heavy for me to move. Will you help me?" Aryla asked without turning around.

"Is he – ?"

"Will you – will you close his eyes for me? I can't."

"Yes."

"I'll call the others. They don't know." Aryla referred to her mother and old aunt and uncle. Finally she turned around and wiped her hands on her apron. Her bravery could last no longer. Her face screwed up in grief.

Rykos ran and took her in his arms. "I'm so sorry. Oh, Aryla."

*

The clouds grew black and heavy as the news spread. The marketplace cleared. The day was suspended.

With this storm came lightning and thunder. The Woodswarder hurried to the fringe of the Ring and sat under thickets of scrub. They grieved. Lor had lived as a legend among them. And Jovia. She was the prize of their protection, and yet she had been lost. Lightning shattered the highest treetops and from them flame leapt until they were drenched.

The Ministration mourned. They sat in darkness split by light and in silence interrupted in reply. None had given up the hope of Jovia's recovery. Surely she would return to her duties, how couldn't she? Jovia was the soul of the city. Their lamentation was great.

The Genexus wore no color. Little ones clambered

into their parents' arms and older children did their best to appear strong. Every flash and thunderous response terrified them, all except Axl who danced in the far fields and vacant pathways. Jovia's passing was felt strongly, but differently, among the Genexus. She was more than the soul of the city to them. She was tangible, the substantiation of everything that they believed and in which they felt secure.

How could life continue? Not as it had. What would it be like?

And Boz. Few understood how revered he was by all. He shared with everyone a personal relationship that was his or hers alone. Boz' simple wisdom, his wink and his smile, were as frequently sought out as his sweets.

Now Rykos would wear his white apron. The city would renew itself in balance and promise. It was a gift to a waiting generation, the passing of an elder. According to popular belief, such exchanges were facilitated by the ether. "'Ether' you live or die," Boz often quipped. None of them, Rykos, Ava or Thayn, had reason to question his claim.

No clever words, however, offered themselves to Arlos' parents. His death was a mystery. "It wasn't his time," his mother told whomever she met. There was no explanation, no comfort.

*

The storms abated. Jovia, Boz and Arlos were taken to the temple. Ministration sat with them. Preparations for their funerals, to be held the following day, had already begun.

*

At dusk, gates in the Wooden Wall opened on either side of the Fallow Field. Cyrll's captains bore Lor to a simple shrine, initiating a somber procession, a Rotation of the Ring. Woodswarder, simultaneously and slowly, walked in the same direction, finding along the way as dry a branch as they could. By the first gate they entered the Fallow Field and, from afar, they paid their respects to Jovia and Boz. At his feet they lamented Lor's passing and, branch by branch, built his funeral pyre. The Woodswarder left by the second gate and continued until they returned to the very spot where they had begun the Rotation. They honored the dead without compromising protection of the city.

As the Rotation of the Ring concluded, Cyrll lit Lor's pyre. It spat and crackled. The High Warden offered a final prayer and departed. The night was nearly spent. By evening he would return.

*

141

At dawn, Genexus filled the temple, their numbers overflowing into the Great Path. Well-wishers chanted ancient verses of Kala. Seldom had such a ceremony honored more than a single passing soul. Here were three, one revered, one celebrated and one so young – a life cut short.

Their pyres were lit. As the wood burst into flame, above the rhythmic chanting of the Genexus and the Ministration, Arlos' mother wailed.

*

After they cooled, Elyda collected the ashes of the departed. That night she walked deep into the Fallow Field among patches of flowering herb and laid her burden to rest. Cyrll joined her, scattering Lor's ashes. The High Minister and High Warden of Eator greeted each other with a grim hug before returning to their respective domains.

*

A next day came, and then another. The weather cleared and, for the greater population, routines of the city resumed. Rykos and Aryla were married. Thayn and Ava performed various duties according to their station. They all learned new ways.

CHAPTER ELEVEN
Many dreams

For Thayn came a period of unexpected unhappiness. Attempting to reason it out, he realized that, until now, Lor had been his referent. When not *with* him, it was *from* him that Thayn strayed. He returned to the High Camp, locating the distinctive tree with shaggy bark, to find another old steward had already claimed Lor's former space as his own, weaving new walls.

For the time being, a thicket of thorny scrub where the Woodswarder had weathered the recent storm, he decided, would serve Thayn as home. Unless –

*

Kaden, Owan and Jad shared a long, low bower along the edge of the carvers' clearing. They had become friends shortly after Kaden's arrival. Now the healing of their arms bound them together. In their present condition none of them could carry out duties

143

of the Ring, their arms in slings.

Those who had witnessed their strange altercation attended to them, bringing them food and brown berries that induced calm and drowsiness. Kaden, Owan and Jad lay in the soft mulch of their bower, slept and healed.

Thayn decided to pay Jad a visit. He stooped in the bower doorway, a sprig of brown berries pinched between his thumb and forefinger.

Owan and Kaden stirred. Jad rubbed his sleepy eyes, delighted to see Thayn. "Come in."

Kaden and Owan reacted to Thayn's visit in opposite ways. Kaden was aloof and remained in the back of the bower. Owan, meanwhile, wouldn't leave Thayn alone. "Let me see your arm. I wonder why it didn't break. Did it hurt? Ours did, right, Jad? Mine *still* hurts. So does Kaden's."

Kaden snorted.

"Funny how much you look like your father. And your uncle, too, because they're twins, right? I think that's just amazing. No wonder Kaden couldn't tell you apart."

Kaden abruptly left the bower.

"Wait. Where are you going?" Owan hurried after him. Thayn and Jad shared a smile until they heard a cry and a thud. Owan returned with Kaden, supporting him. "He tried to climb a tree."

"Let me be." Kaden returned to the back of the bower, grimacing. He glared at Thayn.

"Will you talk to him?" Owan asked Jad. "He won't listen to me."

Thayn had planned to propose to Jad an alternate place for him to convalesce. He imagined himself taking care of Jad. Instead, after looking from Thayn to Kaden and back again, Jad shrugged. "I'll try."

Now Thayn hadn't the chance to ask. "I need to go." He left and never went back.

*

For Thayn, the failed visit to Jad's bower was as devastating as the passing of Lor or Arlos. It felt the same. Thayn returned to his thicket of scrub and decided that he liked it there. Flowers grew everywhere, blue and deeply throated. A small recess was room enough for him to sit and sleep – and think.

Just as well that Jad hadn't joined him, he further decided. After all, Jovia's expectations of him would demand his full attention. Jad would have been a distraction. Thayn reviewed everything that Jovia taught him. He repeated incantations in his head, whispered them to himself and wrote them in the air. Although

145

Jovia shared repeatedly a hope that her words would never make sense, Thayn wanted to understand them. As it was, they were merely sounds strewn together.

For the first time – and not the last – his uncle's words – Arlos' words – returned to haunt him. "Why do you suppose you've come this far, you fool?"

What did they mean?

Thayn reviewed the situation. Arlos, inexplicably, was dead. His appearance in the Ring was phantasmic. Kaden hated Thayn. And Jad – Thayn didn't want to think about him now.

*

Below, as if the canopy had slipped upside down, the grasslands spread away to meet the distant sky. Thayn looked out from his perch high in a tree. He served as a scout. The clouds played shadow tag upon the waves of grass. Thayn marveled at countless little woods scattered everywhere – and nearby mountains.

His outpost was hidden among saplings along the edge of the Ring. From a tower high in the middle of the sector a communicator scanned his mind. Thayn could feel him. Communicators saw what their scouts saw. In this case, it was nothing but the wind.

*

Grasses met the tapering fringe and mingled with

146

an understory of shrubs and ferns through which grew younger trees. Older, greater trees reached up to form the higher arches of the Ring.

In the deepest shadows grew small patches of berries. These weren't the common bushes that sprawled everywhere and yielded red berries that relaxed and aroused. These cultivated bushes produced berries of other colors. Some enhanced communication skills. Others actualized physical potential and a variety of mental powers. One color was instant death. Differences in shading were subtle. Few could interpret them all. None abused them.

Tending the bushes was next on Thayn's duty cycle. They grew in patches isolated from one another. The bushes were compact and their leaves small and waxy. Daily, Thayn examined every leaf. If white scale appeared, the communicator would instruct him to destroy the entire patch.

*

Little other fruit grew in the Ring. Every morning carts of foodstuffs were wheeled to the sector towers. They came from the city. Succulent stalks grown in the fields and baked goods were most popular. Other fruits, mushrooms and herbs were available, too.

Carts laden with goods were pushed by Genexus

147

along the outer paths at dawn and left outside the sector gates. Empty carts left overnight were taken back to the city. Attending to the carts was also on Thayn's cycle of duties.

*

The clearings offered Thayn little diversion. None of the other Woodswarder, he realized, compared to Jad. Thayn visited the carvers' clearing several times but, because of Kaden's hatred, avoided the bower from which he hoped in vain that Jad might emerge.

After every unsuccessful visit Thayn returned to his thicket and wondered if he were some kind of fraud. He ate too many red berries and over-thought the situation. The question, "Why do you suppose you've come this far, you fool?" continued to vex him. Why had Arlos appeared to him? To lead him into the grasslands? Where – to Vok? Thayn wondered if Vok had influenced his own Choosing. Voices from behind the Third Door had cried out to him. Was he meant to be an Outcast?

Added to that was a sense of responsibility that Thayn felt in light of Jovia's teachings. Taken together Thayn felt overwhelmed, unsupported and absolutely, positively sorry for himself. Except when on duty, he avoided others. Nobody seemed to notice.

148

Thayn had sudden shifts in feelings. One moment he hated Jad. The next moment Jad was blameless and everything was Kaden's fault.

*

A dream recurred. Jovia, Lor and Boz sat around a table. They spoke to one another, highly animated, but Thayn couldn't hear them. He awoke in a sweat.

The next night Thayn heard their voices, but he couldn't understand what they were saying. Jovia appeared younger. Thayn suspected that relief from her previous duties agreed with her. Lor seemed more substantial in Thayn's dream than he had in life. He had an assurance, a natural authority that Thayn had never noticed. Boz was the most transformed. He wasn't the jolly, winking market vendor that Thayn remembered. He was astute and persistent.

They repeated their conversation. Again Thayn heard words but he couldn't understand them. Finally Boz spoke more clearly. He said, "Rykos must push the cart."

Familiar voices chanted, softly and without interruption " – expect you to figure it out we expect you to figure it out we – "

Jovia began, "Ava – " Thayn leaned forward to hear her better – and woke up. He heard only the wind

149

in the trees. What, Thayn wondered, was Jovia going to say? And what did Boz mean?

*

Thayn's dream recurred every night. Boz repeated himself and familiar chanting resumed " – expect you to figure it out we expect you to figure it out we – "

At last, Jovia interrupted, "Ava must open the wall."

*

That morning Thayn waited inside a sector gate for carts of goods from the city. He heard Genexus arrive, speaking softly and good-naturedly among themselves. As Thayn retrieved a cart he watched the Genexus retreat along the path, bright spots of color. Bringing up the rear was Rykos.

*

" – you to figure it out we expect you to figure it out we expect – " Thayn's dream continued. Boz and Jovia repeated themselves.

At last, Lor advised Thayn, "Do not be misled by the expectations of others."

*

Perhaps, as Rykos' neighbor, Thayn might have lived a happier life. He sat in his thicket and explored his loneliness. What had happened to him? Whose fault was it? Certainly, it wasn't his. He couldn't help it if Arlos died. He couldn't help it if Kaden hated him. He couldn't help it if he loved Jad.

Wait. Thayn reconsidered his remonstrations. "I can't help it if – *I – love –* Jad?" Thayn recognized, at last, Vok's words for what they really were, an instance of cruel and simple trickery. He attempted to cast Thayn among the unloving in his own thinking so that, as an Outcast, he might join his uncle.

*

Morning sunlight slanted through the canopy. Jad awoke with an irresistible urge to take a walk. Singing softly to himself, he traveled various paths, hoping to meet a cart along his way.

Jad passed the tree where he and Thayn first met. Standing within its slanting branches with a sweetloaf under one arm, Thayn whispered repeatedly an incantation until Jad arrived and interrupted him. "You brought me here? How?"

"Jovia's teachings."

"Why?"

"I have something of yours I want to return."

"What?"

Thayn put his hand behind Jad's neck. "Here." He kissed him.

*

That afternoon while Kaden and Owan slept, Jad watched sunlight shimmer against the bower wall and thought about his morning with Thayn.

So Tylos found them. He smiled. "I wish I didn't come in haste."

Kaden roused.

"Cyrll wishes to speak with you," Tylos informed him.

Kaden jumped to his feet. "I'm ready."

He and Tylos left.

Owan sat up. "Who was that?" he asked sleepily, rubbing his eyes.

"Tylos," Jad told him. "Cyrll summoned Kaden."

"What?" Owan exclaimed. "Come on."

*

Kaden followed Tylos into the pavilion. Tylos took his place with the captains and Kaden stood facing them. Cyrll picked a waterfruit from the dais and threw it. Kaden caught it with the hand of the arm that had broken.

"Good," Cyrll said. "It's been some time since we spoke. Healing time."

Kaden squared his jaw and his expression sharpened.

Cyrll continued, "We've made you welcome in our city. Elyda's goal, however, is to liberate yours. We're in need of greater details. Not lightly, we ask you – "

"I'm ready now," Kaden interrupted.

Cyrll smiled. "Preparations are underway. Tylos requests to accompany you, but I've refused him. His duties are here."

"I know of someone willing to take my place," Tylos suggested. "He's sharp-eyed and – "

Owan rushed into the pavilion. "Here I am."

" – enthusiastic," Tylos concluded.

"I approve." Cyrll waited, smiling. "I imagined a party of three."

"Jad?" called Owan. There was no answer.

Cyrll looked at Kaden.

"Yes," Kaden agreed, "Jad."

Jad entered the pavilion. He looked conflicted.

Cyrll regarded him. "This will be a mission to gather information. We don't know what you'll encounter. There will be risk. Do you accept?"

Jad hesitated. "I'm a Woodsward," he replied.

"Provisions are available in Tylos' tower. Leave when you're ready, but advise me."

"Of course," Kaden promised. He, Owan and Jad

left to make ready.

Kaden was eager to see what had been prepared. Having made the journey once, he wanted to make sure that certain items had been included. They entered Tylos' quarters at the base of the tower, a large circular structure situated around the tallest tree in the sector. It was framed with saplings and tented with woven vine. Ladders reached to meet the bridging overhead and others reached higher still to the communicator's platform.

On a table were items for Kaden's mission. Sacks were filled with fruit and hardloaf. Cloaks of a special weave would offer them protection from both the eye and the elements. Someone planned well to include knives, a bag of flint, ointment to protect against the sun and, best of all, thick leggings.

*

Owan was excited and couldn't stop talking. Admittedly, he couldn't imagine what the world would be like outside the Ring. He had spent so many hours scanning the grasslands. He knew how they waved in the wind, how they withered and renewed themselves. He had never ventured more than a few steps into them. And now to go to Yutor. He had heard of other cities since his Choosing and believed in them, but never thought to see such things himself. "How will we find our way? Will we encounter others? What will happen when we get there?"

Kaden smiled at Owan. "We'll see."

Jad frowned. "When do we leave?"

"I'm ready now," Kaden replied.

"So am I," Owan added.

"I have to see Thayn."

"Quickly – please. I've been ready too long."

*

Jad hurried along branch and bridging through the canopy until he dropped to the floor of the Ring. Within a clearing Thayn tended a patch of berries. He sang to himself as he inspected the leaves, his expression full of renewed hopefulness.

Thayn's expression drained upon hearing Jad's unexpected news. He stood for a moment in silence, unable to move or think what to say.

"Come with us. I'll ask Tylos to ask Cyrll and Kaden."

"No," Thayn refused at the mention of Kaden's name.

Jad hesitated for a moment longer. "They're waiting," he said. "One last time, then – "

"Our last time won't be now," Thayn managed.

"We'll be all right."

Jad kissed him softly. "I have to go."

*

Cyrll joined the Woodswarder as they left Tylos' tower and escorted them to the fringe of the Ring. Elyda reached into their minds and wished them well. "I'll be with you," she promised. Kaden, Owan and Jad departed Eator.

*

Thayn scarcely had time to regret Jad's unexpected departure. That night he slept fitfully as pieces of his dream flooded him. Above the incessant chant, Boz, Jovia and Lor repeated their declarations, louder and louder, until they seemed to scream.

Thayn awoke repeatedly.

A new dream took shape. Kaden's arm met Jad's and it broke. *Crack.* Jad's arm met Owan's and it broke. *Crack.* This time Owan's met an arm that Thayn didn't recognize. *Crack.* Another appeared to meet it. *Crack.* And another.

Thayn watched in horror. Something was missing in his dream. Where was *he*? It was Thayn's arm that was supposed to stop what now continued. *Crack.* The arms became younger and younger.

His first dream returned. Boz, Jovia and Lor

screamed, "Rykos must push the cart. Ava must open the wall. Do not be misled by the expectations of others."

" – you to figure it out we expect you – " the chanting shifted in cadence as the thin outline of a hand appeared in the air and opened into a pool of light " – to figure it out we expect you – to figure it out we expect you – to figure it out we expect you – *now*."

"Oh." Only half awake, Thayn scrambled to his feet. He made his way quickly to the nearest sector gate. A Woodsward returned carts to the path. Thayn offered to help. As he pushed the last cart through the gate, the Woodsward turned to thank Thayn, but he was gone.

*

Men of the city, Rykos among them, collected the empty carts that morning. He lagged behind his fellows as they reached the Great Path. Joking and laughing, they pointed their carts toward the marketplace. Instead, Rykos pushed his cart across the Great Path and through the shadows all the way to the Center.

The thin outline of a hand appeared in the wall. It opened. Rykos pushed his cart into a little room.

Thayn hopped out of it. "Ava?"

"Hush."

PART THREE

CHAPTER TWELVE
Kaden's mission

Generations before Jovia's ministration a young Woodsward visited his family over the wall of an outer path. He served as a scout high in the trees, proud to be a Woodsward and even prouder of himself. He so wanted to impress his family that he violated his oath and spoke to them of the grasslands.

For most Genexus the world ended at the Wooden Wall. Woodswarder lived beyond it and guarded them. The woods, young Genexus learned from their elders, extended to the very edge of existence. Woodswarder and Genexus visited together freely at that time, but by oath the Woodswarder didn't speak of many things.

The young Woodsward's family was astonished to hear that the world wasn't as they had been taught. They told others in the city about the grasslands. It was Forbidden Knowledge. Ministration, as a warning to all, closed their minds. From that time on, Woods-warder avoided contact with the Genexus. Owan was reminded of that story as into those very grasslands he, Kaden and Jad set foot.

Woodswarder and Ministration learned from their mentors an account of the world different from what they were taught as young Genexus. According to For-bidden Knowledge time began when Kala fell into the desert. He became the great body of land on which they lived. His sturdy ribs and mountainous shoulders surrounded the grasslands.

The Woodswarder took broad strides through the grass, slicing a path that filled again with the wind. Owan and Jad looked back at the Ring. Everywhere around Eator grew other woods that looked alike, iso-lated clumps of trees.

Ahead a scatter of trees wandered down from the ribbed highlands. Although out of their way, the trees would offer the Woodswarder a measure of protection. Kaden's previous journey had been across open land and the sun had blistered his skin. Although their trav-eling cloaks shielded their shoulders, and despite thick leggings, Kaden feared the unfriendly eyes of Outcasts and rats.

Owan heard water. He ran ahead of the others to

discover a stream within the trees. A short falls fed a pool that swelled against a smooth rim of rock. Water skimmed over it, gurgling and swirling.

In the city, water came either from pipes or from troughs. Owan and Jad had never seen it running wild. They pointed at the bubbles, eddies and reflections.

Kaden, who came to know the river on his earlier journey, didn't like the water at all. Nevertheless, he decided uneasily, "We'll stay here tonight."

They slipped out of their cloaks. Almost at once Owan and Jad were in the pool. Owan splashed about and sent water everywhere.

Kaden stretched their cloaks between slender trees to make a shelter. "Can you see me?"

"Barely."

"Join us," Owan called. He splashed water at Jad as Kaden came out of the shelter.

"You're either very brave or very foolish," Kaden scolded him. "We don't know what ears and eyes are upon us."

Jad pulled himself out of the pool and wrung out his bristlecloth. He slipped into the shelter.

Owan chased after him, laughing.

"Don't drip on my drawing," Kaden called after them.

"Careful," Jad admonished Owan.

Kaden made his way to the edge of the pool. He washed himself at its side, cupping water in his hands and pouring it down himself. When he returned to the shelter, Jad sat on the ground and Owan stood over him, tempting Jad with a sprig of red berries.

Jad looked at Kaden and shrugged.

"You *are* fools," Kaden whispered. He looked into the trees. "Quietly – oh – "

Owan tackled Kaden with a laugh, bringing him down to the floor. He pushed a berry against Kaden's lips and it burst.

The Woodswarder relaxed. Owan opened his pack and pulled out greenfruit. The berries were potent and the greenfruit was sweet and slick.

*

By twilight they lay around a drawing that Kaden had scratched into the sand. It was a map. Kaden re-traced its lines and circles. Thayn would have recognized it as a small part of the same map of the land that he often drew. "This knowledge is a gift from Elyda. It's a thought she gave me to guide our way."

The circles farther apart were Eator and Yutor. A middle circle between two lines was an island. The two lines were the river. They met a thinner line, the

161

stream along which the Woodswarder made camp, at an angle. "We're here," Kaden indicated.

He proposed with his finger a path from the stream to the river, crossing it above the island. His finger continued to the circle that was Yutor. This wasn't the route that he had taken last time.

The moon rose as Kaden retold his tale and the sky grew silver. Kaden squared his jaw and his blue eyes chilled. Owan and Jad had heard his story already but, given their present situation, they listened with re-newed interest.

*

Kaden's flight took him from Yutor to the river. He scrambled through patches of tall grass to hide from Vok's army and roaming Outcasts. The blades of grass were sharp and nicked his skin.

"I had heard of the river in tales told by my elders and I thought I saw it once in the distance as, from my post in a tall tree, I guarded Yutor. The river turned out to be very different than what I imagined. Instead of a magical, mystical place, it ran past as a great ob-stacle, wet and wide.

"Sturdy posts on opposite banks of the river sup-ported a thick rope that was stretched between them. At first I didn't understand their purpose, nor that I looked at an island.

"I walked into the water. The river was deep and its bed was slick. To my astonishment, the opposite shore seemed to float upstream. The current, already strong, strengthened with every step.

"Luck was with me. I stumbled upon a submerged pathway of slippery stone that had once, I learned, supported a bridge."

Kaden was luckier than he knew. He had avoided the nearer of two fords that provided access to a wretched community. Both fords were frequented by Outcasts who, at present, called the place home.

The island didn't offer the Outcasts much. They still needed to hunt the grasslands for vermin to eat. Reminiscent of a city, the island was circular in shape and was protected, in this case, by the river. Known as Tordawn, it was coveted by roving bands of Outcasts that fought for control. Tordawn changed hands often. To possess it, rivals would do terrible things.

"My luck continued. I heard voices and hid behind a pile of driftwood. Two grizzled women hurried past me. They shouted nonsense to each other, shoving a scrawny young man back and forth between them.

"Skirting the center of the island, sneaking through reeds and brush, I continued on my way. I reached the other ford. It was at this point I realized I was on an island. Again, two thick posts on opposite banks supported a rope stretched between them. I watched from behind a bush as Outcasts used the rope to guide rafts across the river."

At dusk the cloudy sky darkened quickly. Kaden crept to the landing but, upon hearing voices, returned to his hiding place. Traffic continued across the river by torchlight. Despite his best effort to remain alert, he was exhausted and fell into a troubled sleep.

"I awoke to a starry gray sky and a thin moon. I attempted the ford again, slipping onto a raft and pushing it into the water. My luck turned. I saw shapes on the opposite shore. Outcasts had launched a raft in my direction. I let go of the rope and slipped off my raft, trying to stand up, but the river was too deep. I surrendered myself to the current, clinging to the raft as it swirled away.

"I quickly learned to propel the raft by kicking my feet and, with my arms, I guided myself to the far shore. Downstream, away from the paths surrounding Tordawn, I pulled the raft out of the water."

Along the river the grasslands were infested with rats. Outcasts hunted and ate them. The rats needed to eat, too. They ate other rats, and Outcasts who had grown too old, infirm or unfortunate to escape them when the balance tilted.

A rat sank its teeth into Kaden's leg. As he hopped on one leg to yank it from the other, more rats attacked. This time he bolted, smacking rats from his legs, running until he no longer heard their squeaking.

"Where was I? And Eator? I knew it lay near the highlands of Kala, but where? I prayed I would sense its energy and, again, I ran.

"The morning sun was hot. I continued, exhausted but determined. At last the Ring of Eator appeared in the distance and Owan spotted me."

*

Kaden finished his story. Jad smiled. Owan nodded, half asleep.

*

The next morning the Woodswarder refreshed themselves in the pool. Kaden waded this time to his knees. After a quick meal of waterfruit and hardloaf they dismantled their shelter, packed up camp and resumed their journey.

The stream cut through crags and tumbles of rock. Trees grew wherever they could through broken stone and stepped along the course offering shade and protection. Fed by springs, the water widened along the way.

Ahead the course meandered, trapping a finger of grasslands within its bend. A trail trampled through the grass disappeared under the far wall of trees. The men slowed their pace and kept aware of where the trail would cross their path.

The marker that they chose, a stand of trees with red leaves, was soon upon them. The trail was on its other side. Kaden scanned the canopy. Thick branches reached high. Owan and Jad followed his look.

The Woodswarder sprang into the trees. The light through their leaves fluttered as a breeze embraced them. Kaden, Owan and Jad climbed high, finding forks from which to observe the surrounding area. The view was magnificent.

On the other side of the stream the grasslands continued to the distant shoulders of Kala. Upstream rose the ribbed highlands. Looking back in the direction that they had come, the Woodswarder thought that they could see the Ring of Eator rising from the grasslands, but there were so many clumps of trees from which to choose that it was only a guess, and none of them guessed the same. How easy to feel vulnerable so far from home, they realized.

Owan saw two figures walking along the grassy

trail. "They're moving away." He detected no other movement in the grasslands. Below them they heard nothing but gurgling water.

The stream straightened beyond a last meander but the trees didn't follow. Rock disappeared and grass grew up to the water's edge. In the distance the river stretched like a great blue ribbon. Downstream, in its middle, was Tordawn.

The men spoke in low tones.

"Let's cross there," advised Kaden, pointing upstream. "The current is strong and we need to avoid the island."

"Should we walk across the grasslands," Owan asked, pointing up the river, "or follow the water?"

"After we lose the cover of the trees, let's go the shorter way."

"Look," Jad exclaimed, pointing.

A figure on the path hurried toward them. Kaden and Owan regarded it curiously.

Kaden asked, "What's she doing here?"

Owan replied, "She? I see an old man. Wait a minute, he's my – "

"Thayn – ?" Jad yelled. He scrambled down the tree.

"No," Kaden called after him. "Wait."

It was too late. Jad had already dropped to the ground. "Thayn?"

"Yes," a voice yelled back.

An old woman hurried toward Jad, a powerful witch, as the Woodswarder soon learned. Few saw her as she truly was, and by everyone she was seen differently. To Kaden she was his sister, and to Owan his grandfather, both of them beloved. "She's a changer," Kaden whispered.

"He is?" Owan whispered in return.

"A witch. And to Jad she looks like Thayn."

"How?"

"I've heard stories, but I never thought she was real. She makes her appearance out of memories." Kaden's expression hardened.

"Oh." Owan's expression softened. He looked down at Jad with greater concern than before. "What will he – *she* – do to him?"

"I don't know."

Jad's face was wide with excitement as he and the witch met and hugged. She held him tightly for a moment, then pushed him away, holding Jad at arm's length. "Yes, you'll do nicely."

As if in response, Jad flinched. He ran his fingers across his forehead and smiled. His expression, from then on, never changed.

The witch pretended to explain, "I've fallen and hit my head, you see. I remember nothing as I should. Follow me – " she prompted him.

" – Jad – "

" – of course – *Jad* – and tell me everything I've forgotten." The witch led Jad away.

"I don't think he saw me," Owan observed.

"I don't think she can see," Kaden replied. "She's blind. We need to follow carefully and quietly. Don't make a sound."

They worked their way through the treetops. The witch limped below them along a route that she obviously knew well. Jad had to duck and bend to avoid branches and stumps.

In time they reached a gray grove of dead trees. Kaden and Owan dropped to the ground from the last healthy tree. They followed on foot.

A hollow in the middle of the grove was her home. Kaden and Owan slipped from one ragged tree trunk to the next until they were repelled by a sweet stench.

"Oh," Owan exclaimed.

"Quiet," Kaden warned.

"I'm so glad you've come, Jad," the witch cooed. "I've been helpless without you." Jad tilted his head and they kissed.

Owan stifled another cry.

Again, it was too late. Frowning, the witch looked in Kaden's direction. "I know you're there, brother. I sense you. You do well not to come too close. Leave this one, I warn you, or I'll destroy him."

CHAPTER THIRTEEN
Tordawn

The witch gestured around her at the bones and carcasses of rats in various stages of decay. "You'll carry all of this away. I'll show you where to throw it." Jad would rid the witch's hollow of its squalor. He filled his arms with an indescribable mass and she led the way out of the gray grove and into the woods in a new direction.

Kaden and Owan followed through the treetops. The witch continued to appear to them as Kaden's sister and Owan's grandfather. She stopped and turned. "Are you still here, brother? Heed my warning."

A rat ran into the path, diverting her. She pointed at it and whispered. A pulse of light escaped her fingertips and stunned the creature.

Jad dropped his load and retrieved it for her. The witch licked her lips. Her spell was weak and the rat

171

revived. "Watch me. Learn to do this." A last squeak was cut short as she skinned the rat with her teeth.

"Oh." Owan was almost sick.

Its filet was meager. "Bother." Despite her penury, she was a picky eater and tossed most of the rat away.

Jad and the witch resumed their work. She guided him poorly and it seemed to take forever. Every time Kaden and Owan grew too near, she threatened them.

*

That night Jad and the witch returned to her hollow with fresh rats and prepared to skin them. "I can't watch," Owan grimaced.

"Neither can I." Kaden and Owan sought refuge in the nearest healthy tree outside the grave grove.

"What'll we do?" Owan asked rhetorically.

"Pray to Kala," Kaden snorted. They spent an uncomfortable night.

*

The next morning Owan asked, "Does she know how she appears to us?"

"Why?"

"She calls us 'brother'. I don't think she senses me. Or she senses us as one person."

"Or she calls all men 'brother'." Owan frowned at

the idea until Kaden added, "All I know is she can appear differently to people at the same time."

Owan brightened again. "Let's split up. It's worth a try." They made plans.

Jad continued his task. It had been a long time since the gray grove had been defouled and it took him most of the day. Finally the job was done and he and the witch rested.

Kaden skirted the hollow, standing behind several ragged trees. The witch felt him. His sister's voice asked, "Are you still here?"

"Yes."

"You feel different to me. Why?" She took several steps toward him.

Owan rushed the hollow from the other side. He reached Jad just as the witch whirled around. "What are you doing?" Owan's grandfather barked.

To Kaden, "Stop or I'll destroy him." His sister raised her arm and pointed toward Jad.

Jad reached his hands to his head. "Oh."

Kaden shouted, "Owan, leave him."

"No," Jad moaned.

Kaden and Owan ran away in opposite directions. They met in the treetops and spoke in dispirited tones.

"We'll have to try again," Owan sighed.

"We'll have to think of something else," Kaden concluded. "We can't kill Jad to free him."

"And we can't go on without him."

Kaden said nothing in reply.

"Kaden?" He and Owan spent another uncomfortable night.

*

The following morning they tried again. This time Owan rode on Kaden's shoulders. If they could get closer to Jad before they separated, then Kaden would divert the witch while Owan rescued Jad.

They were about to execute their plan when others stepped into the hollow. Tall and broad, they were repulsive to the eye, and snickered.

"No, not you," the witch shrieked in their direction. Kaden and Owan heard laughter behind them, too. More men stood there, as tall and repulsive as the others. Outcasts surrounded them.

One of them approached Jad. Kaden called to him, "No. She'll destroy his mind."

"She no longer has the power." A pulse of light from her fingertips smacked the Outcast squarely, but he barely flinched. "Only fools fear her. We come, now and again, to make her fools our own."

The witch appeared to the Woodswarder as the

wrinkled old woman that she was, colorless, as if she had been left out in the sun too long. Her hair, in patches, stuck out in odd directions. "I haven't had two days of service out of him," she complained.

One of the Outcasts held his hand to the witch's neck. "Release him or – " She complied.

Jad looked at the old woman. "Who are you?"

The Outcasts laughed.

"Where's Thayn?" His expression returned as Jad looked around at everyone. "What's happening?"

Prodded by the Outcasts, Kaden and Owan joined Jad as captives. The Outcasts' laughter continued.

"It's not fair," the witch sniveled. The Outcast who threatened the old woman pushed her away. She twirled around, her fingertips waving in front of her. Another Outcast pushed her, and then another.

She stumbled.

"No," Kaden objected.

They stopped. The tallest among the Outcasts approached Kaden.

"Really? You defend her?" He smiled. "Or do we bother you?"

His teeth were green and black with slime and decay. He held his knife to Kaden's throat and positioned their faces together.

175

"Maybe this will seal your lips." He licked them.

The Outcasts pushed Kaden, Owan and Jad ahead of them out of the hollow.

"You'll pay," the witch yelled after them. "Some-day you'll pay."

*

The last thing that Jad remembered was seeing Thayn on a grassy path. Now it was days later. What happened? After binding their captives' wrists behind their backs and stringing them together, the Outcasts alternated the Woodswarder among them and prodded them along the same path into the grasslands. They wore the Woodswarder's cloaks and leggings now.

Their progress was interrupted by rats. The Outcasts beat them, too infrequently, with sticks. The rats were fearless and the legs of the Woodswarder bled.

The party advanced from the stream to the river-bank opposite Tordawn. They stood at the ford that Kaden had attempted on his previous journey, its rope stretching from one side to the other.

The Woodswarder were put on separate rafts, two Outcasts apiece to navigate and guard them. Kaden glanced at the current as if he might jump, but his guard, the tallest Outcast, pulled out his knife again and licked his lips.

"Thayn," Jad cried, looking into the water. A face looked back at him. The Outcasts stared at Jad. So did Kaden. Jad lowered his head and called no further attention to himself.

After crossing the river, the Woodswarder were pushed off the rafts and strung together again. "I'm losing my mind," Jad admitted to the others.

"No," Kaden whispered. "I saw him, too."

*

They followed a sandy path to the interior of the island. A stand of stunted trees with feathery leaves grew there. Under them, driftwood shacks made up an unsavory city. Outcasts, some of them masters and most of them slaves, stood in windows and doorways. The Woodswarder were led to a disagreeable room, the first of several in a row, and shoved into it. Two Outcasts stood guard outside the open doorway.

Interior windows connected the row. In the last room Owan could see the tallest of their captors speaking with a fat Outcast. He pointed in their direction. Music came from that room, a low beating of drums.

The Fat One produced a sheath and from it pulled a long blade. The men disappeared. They reappeared in the open doorway. The Fat One looked at the Woodswarder.

"Who are you?" Kaden asked.

"Your words insult me," the Fat One replied. He sheathed the blade and, in exchange for the Woodswarder, gave the knife to the tall, smiling Outcast who followed the Fat One back to the far room where the drums were beating.

Owan saw something move in the next room. A young man emerged out of a pile of rags. He was lean with tangled red hair and wore rat skins around his waist. As if his surroundings were all too familiar, he looked at nothing. He stretched and took a drink from a basin. Then, with a glance at Owan, he announced, "You'll be sorry you met me."

"Why?" Owan asked.

Kaden and Jad joined Owan at the window.

"Because," the young man replied, "you have to fight me."

"What?" Owan exclaimed.

An Outcast guarding the doorway snarled at Owan to be quiet until passers-by distracted him.

"What do you mean I have to fight you?"

"You've been captured," the young man explained. "I have to choose one of you and fight you. The winner stays – "

" – where – ?"

" – alive."

The guards came into the room. One of them called to the young man, "Which one?"

The young man pointed at Owan. The guards smiled at him, then took Kaden and Jad and bound them to the opposite wall.

"Why did you pick me?" Owan asked.

An odd expression flickered across the young man's face. "Because I think I can beat you."

*

The arrival of new prisoners was a major event among the Outcasts. The Chosen One would retain his status with victory or succumb to humiliation and defeat. He was kept as a living trophy, a tribute to the fickle nature of fortune and power. It was an entertainment that the Fat One offered his community.

Like a caged animal they watched him through his open door. As the Fat One's prize he lived well, but always under the direct threat of the next prisoner to be brought before him.

It was determined that Owan would be his new opponent. The community watched him, too, preparing for a feast and a fight. Owan and the Chosen One moved about their respective rooms freely. Kaden and Jad, however, remained bound to the walls.

"I bet on this new one," a skinny woman decided.

"No," her stout companion disagreed, "I bet on our boy Fildor. He's beat all his challengers, hasn't he?"

"Fildor's getting too scrawny. He should eat more meat."

"Smile," one of Fildor's guards called to Owan, "at death incarnate."

"How poetic," one of Owan's guards replied, "now shut your face."

"Shut up yourself."

The two guards attacked each other, rolling about on the ground, flailing. Other Outcasts egged them on until the Fat One emerged to break it up.

Owan glanced at Fildor who curled his lips.

*

For days Fildor glared at Owan through the window. The Outcasts of the island continued to gawk at them and make bets. Other fights broke out between those who didn't agree.

Food was brought to the Woodswarder. It was rat meat. To Fildor the guards brought mushroom caps, his latest privilege as the Fat One's prize.

"Where did they get those?" Kaden asked as he saw the mushrooms go by.

The Woodswarder ate nothing.

Owan studied Fildor. Although he appeared half-starved, he was muscular. His hands were large. For some reason Owan sensed in Fildor a temper that could quickly rise through passion into rage. "I don't want to fight you," Owan finally admitted, more to himself than anyone.

Fildor shrugged, then nodded at Kaden and Jad. "I don't want to fight him, or him. I picked you."

"Yet I don't want to die." Owan shook his head.

"They do worse now. It's new."

"They – ? I thought you – wait, what's worse than death?"

Fildor came up to the window and spoke softly, intimately. "It used to be a fight to the death. To culminate your humiliation – " his rat skins parted as he reached within them –

Owan's eyes followed. They grew wide with anticipation.

" – I would slit your throat – with this." Fildor produced a crooked knife.

"What happens now?"

"They send you to the new city."

"Where?

"It's horrible, they say."

"What new city?"

"That way," Fildor said, pointing. "The city in the trees."

Instead of death as a penalty, the Fat One traded losers with Yutor for foodstuffs. Already change had come to the island. No longer would its population depend on the balance of rats for survival. Now they could broker slaves instead.

"Let me make sure I understand this. After you – humiliate – me," Owan asked, glancing down again as Fildor returned the knife, "you send me to the city?"

"Yes." Fildor adjusted his rat skins.

"I'm ready."

"What?"

"To fight and go to the city in the trees."

"You're not afraid?"

"I'm brave."

"Where do you come from?" Fildor asked suspiciously.

"We're Woodswarder from Eator."

"The Second Door. I knew it. I wanted to be a Woodsward, too. I've heard of them. The Second Door should have opened for me." Fildor brought his fist down on the ledge of the window.

It splintered. Kaden and Jad, who had dozed off, awoke with a start.

"Why didn't it? How could this have happened? Why didn't the Second Door open?"

The crowd outside murmured in approval at Fildor's seeming display of violence.

Owan noted, "Your temper, perhaps. But now that you tell me about it, I'm glad you want to – fight – me."

"You are?"

"Yes. You don't want to fight my friends – " Owan looked at Kaden and Jad " – because they're stronger than you, or because – ?"

Fildor flushed and whispered, "I want you to fight back."

*

Driftwood stumps and logs defined an arena in a sandy spot near the center of the island. Fires smoked around it. Torches were already lit and the community waited.

Activities in preparation for the upcoming event reached a fevered pitch. Such fights had become the fulcrum upon which the culture of the island balanced. Everyone took sides, and those with nothing of value wagered bragging rights. Time itself was measured relative to the reign of the Chosen One.

The Fat One led the procession. Women followed

him carrying spits of rat meat. They were quickly distributed among the greedy crowd.

Two guards escorted Fildor, the Chosen One. He waved and the crowd cheered. The rest of the guards surrounded his challenger, Owan. He wore rat skins now.

The community cooked their meat over the fires. Sour smoke filled the air. The Fat One ate mushrooms from Yutor.

Boom, boom, boom. The adversaries circled each other to the beat of a drum. *Boom, boom, boom.*

The Fat One nodded. In response, Fildor lunged at Owan with his hands clasped together. A great swing brought them against Owan's jaw.

Owan reeled and fell to the sand.

The crowd roared.

He rolled away quickly as Fildor sprang, missing him. Owan jumped on top of Fildor and spat.

Fildor freed one hand and stuck it in Owan's face. He freed the other and sank it into Owan's stomach. Owan fell back.

Both men rose slowly, staring, and circled each other again. Owan knocked into a driftwood pedestal that held a bowl of greenfruit. It fell. The greenfruit scattered between them.

The crowd whistled and hollered. Owan leapt forward and Fildor fell. Greenfruit smashed everywhere. Fildor fought and Owan fought back, long and hard. They rolled over each other, wresting themselves free and tackling each other repeatedly.

Finally Fildor pinned Owan beneath him and, with an exaggerated cry of victory, slammed himself down again and again. The cheering crowd urged them on until, after a protracted struggle, neither of the competitors moved. Reluctant that the entertainment was over, losers begrudgingly settled their bets and everyone left the arena.

The guards pulled Fildor off Owan and returned them to their rooms. Owan was bound to the wall next to Kaden and Jad.

The Woodswarder would be sold to Yutor.

CHAPTER FOURTEEN
Forsaken places

The broad hallway that ran inside the circumference of the Center narrowed as it passed the kitchens, allowing for a series of storage rooms adjacent to the smithies and marketplace. Thayn stood up in an empty larder facing Ava and Rykos. He tilted his head. Ava stared at nothing, her lips bunched. Rykos looked back and forth between them. "I sense someone in the hallway," Ava whispered.

"I can hear them." Thayn concentrated. "They've come for oilstem."

Ministration located the oilstem that they sought and withdrew. Ava put her hand to the wall and it opened. "Go."

Rykos hesitated as Thayn went through the opening. Ava scolded him, "It won't stay open by itself. Hurry."

They quickly crossed the hallway and Ava opened the opposite wall. They slipped into another storeroom and walked its length.

Ava touched smooth stone in seemingly random spots and the walls melted away. Unexpected passageways revealed themselves. After continuous twists and turns, Rykos wondered if Ava really knew her way.

"I can hear what you're thinking," she replied.

Rykos glanced at Thayn, astonished.

Thayn nodded. "So can I," he added.

"How?" Rykos wondered to himself.

"It's a gift from Jovia."

Ava's thoughts came to Thayn as the voices in his head. Thayn and Ava visited quickly and freely. Rykos stared at them, oblivious to their exchange.

"What I'm about to do," Ava said aloud to Rykos, "I don't do lightly, but it seems only fair. Don't betray us."

"Betray you?"

Holding her fingertips to his forehead, Ava spoke softly and quickly. Her eyes closed and opened again. Rykos' expression changed.

Thayn could feel Rykos' mind burgeon as they continued down a corridor. "How did she do that?" he asked himself. This time both Ava and Rykos could

187

hear his thoughts.

"I've been studying." Already Ava knew how to guide her powers.

Rykos laughed. He would have been afraid, but his new awareness brought with it an understanding that made sense of things. His shoulders squared.

They entered, for the time being, one last chamber. In it were blankets, supplies and food. "Here's what you'll need. Wait until I return. Rest if you can." Ava left.

"Still the boss," Rykos thought.

"Careful. She'll hear you," Thayn said. In regard to Rykos, he observed to himself, "How different he looks."

"She knows she's bossy," Rykos replied aloud. He thought to himself, "You look different, too."

"This will take some getting used to," they shared. They both tried to stop thinking, but it didn't work.

"I wish I were home," Rykos lamented.

"I bet we get in trouble," Thayn feared.

"You and me both." They smiled at each other.

"There are ways to block your mind," Thayn said aloud. "I figured out some of them when – when I heard other thoughts – and Jovia taught me more. Do you want me to show you?"

Rykos considered for a moment. At present his thoughts shuffled too quickly for Thayn to read them easily. "No, not yet," Rykos replied at last.

He opened his mind to Thayn without directing it. Everything that happened to Rykos since their Choosings was available for review, his new life in the city with Aryla.

*

Thayn explored his friend's thoughts. There was curious energy in Rykos' feelings for his wife. Rykos didn't know it yet, but Aryla would have a child. Thayn could *sense* it.

Jovia had taught Thayn well.

Thayn was careful to block most of his own thinking. The story of the Woodsward who spoke too freely to his family haunted him. He selected what to share with Rykos about the Ring and Jad.

*

"Show me now," Rykos requested.

"What?"

"How to block my mind to you. You're doing it well. I can feel it."

With a smile Thayn explained two methods. They practiced.

Thayn did his best to clear his mind of all thought.

189

He tried to think of nothing, but couldn't, so he thought of darkness, or white, or the flame of oilstem, or anything that was singular in nature.

Rykos, instead, flooded his mind with thoughts of everything all at once. He thought of Aryla and the marketplace and how to make mellowpuffs and jellycrips and every type of bread that he could remember. He thought about his family and Aryla's family and how he wanted to start his own family. He thought about his childhood and school and everyone whom he had ever known.

Both made progress against the other's probing. It exhausted Rykos, though, and weariness overcame him. Thayn rested his head against the wall for awhile and watched Rykos doze.

Ava returned. "Are you ready?"

Thayn sprang to his feet. "Oh – almost." He went to the table and selected supplies, stuffing them into a sack that Ava had prepared for him. "Thanks."

Ava, Thayn and Rykos passed back into the adjoining chamber and down another series of halls. They made their way carefully. Ava opened many doorways, avoiding Ministration, and Thayn and Rykos followed her. They reached a familiar chamber of smooth rock. Two of the Doors of Choosing blinked.

The Third Door, sealed, was dull and crooked in its frame.

Thayn and Ava compared their thoughts. Jovia had given them each parts of an incantation. "Are you ready?" Ava asked aloud.

Thayn looked from Rykos to Ava. He had already left them once. Why was it no easier now?

Suddenly Ava looked past him toward the opposite wall. "Thayn, they're coming. Hurry." They twisted their thoughts together. *"Trea abba acca adda."*

As Ava assessed Thayn's thinking she exclaimed, "My, what secrets you keep. You know more than any among the Ministration." Ava's recent studies put into perspective the knowledge that Thayn had gleaned from the Forbidden Room.

The Third Door squared itself with their whisperings. *"Trea abba acca adda,"* they chanted. The Third Door swung open and Thayn sprang through it.

At the very same moment the wall behind Ava and Rykos opened. Elyda, followed by several Monitors, entered the Hall of Choosing. *"Trea baab caac daad,"* she commanded.

The Third Door hesitated for a moment. It shuddered. Ava stopped whispering and the Third Door slammed shut, sinking again into its frame.

191

Elyda cried, "What have you done?"

*

Thayn felt himself sliding along a smooth passage-way. It wasn't steep, but it was slick. He couldn't stay on his feet. As his eyes adjusted to the darkness, he found that he was inside a long tunnel ribbed with arches. Tributaries contributed to a flow of ooze that carried Thayn along. He scrambled to his feet only to slip again.

The smell was overpowering, pungent and earthy. Thayn adjusted to it only because he had no choice. He pulled his cloak around him, glad to be inside it.

After what seemed forever, Thayn arrived at the back of a wide cave into which other tunnels opened. Through a breach in the far wall he could see the sky.

He ran to the edge of the cave. Slime sloughed over its lip. A boulder to one side of the opening was dry. Thayn scrambled up it and took a deep breath.

He squinted against the brightness of the day, blue and yellow light. A vast empty space spread out below him, a basin of sun-bleached scum. Angling away in either direction rose mountainous legs that met knobby peaks before continuing out of sight.

Water from above poured along one side of the cave. Mingling with the ooze and slime, the water carved a trough into the sand that filled with bubbles. The froth stretched wide. Far out between the mountains, it dried along an irregular edge. Then desert spread as far and wide as the eye could see.

Thayn didn't like this place. He hadn't considered exactly where the Third Door might take him, but this certainly wasn't what he expected. Behind him a passageway belched. Thayn resolved that he wouldn't go back the way that he had come.

He looked up. The cliff in which the cave opened was sheer and he could see nothing of the grasslands. He needed to find a way to double back up into the mountains if he wanted to reach them. Yutor was his destination, wasn't it?

Or was everything suddenly less clear to him?

Below him a steep slip of shale fell from the cave. It initiated a path, Thayn discovered, that slanted above the crusty bubbles along the far slopes. It was narrow, barely hugging its way below broken cliffs. The path led away from the waterfall, sadly, in an uninviting direction. A sense of foreboding overwhelmed Thayn. It lasted for only a moment.

He decided to follow the path. Something guided him. Thayn could sense it. Perhaps it was another shred of Jovia's blessing.

He started along the broken shale. With a tremendous belch the floor of the cave filled with a wash of ooze. It swept toward the edge. Thayn hurried and he stumbled. The shale beneath him slid.

The spill of shale stopped only as Thayn neared the surface of the scum. He was afraid to breathe.

After a moment he crawled carefully and with sustained effort back to the path. It angled oddly, slanting sideways. The shale underfoot was loose and Thayn's progress was slow.

He found no immediate opportunity to climb into the mountain. The opposite leg was much gentler, but the wasteland bulged out between it and him. Thayn needed to travel around – or through – it to the other side if he couldn't find a break in the cliffs. Either way, he had to continue.

Or was his resolution waning?

The froth bubbled below him, chalky on top like icing that Boz made before it was thoroughly mixed together. Thayn's way grew steeper. Again the shale spilled and he slipped.

A long white arm reached out of the scum and grabbed for him. "What – ?" Thayn recoiled, pulling his cloak around him. The arm searched for a touch of him. Thayn stared at it, horrified.

He grabbed a piece of shale and threw it into the froth. The arm dived after it. Thayn hurried along his way, sliding and scrambling. Other arms reached after him.

Thayn found a break in the cliff. He crawled up into a steep fissure. After climbing higher he discovered that it led nowhere.

He returned to the path and, dodging another arm, continued as quickly as caution allowed. He found other breaks in the cliff and explored them. They led nowhere, too, and wasted his time, but they offered him some respite, at least, out of arms' reach.

Soon the mountain twisted to its peak and out of sight. Thayn remembered the crooked shape from his map of the land. He needed to find a way up it now. He reconsidered the gentler slopes of the opposite leg. They grew farther away and still the outermost curve of the wasteland reached across the way.

Thayn decided to try one final break in the cliff above the path. It led into a curious depression that was comprised of different rock. One of its faces was smooth. Thayn sensed within it faint energy.

He positioned his fingertips at several different places on the wall of smooth rock and applied his palm. The energy grew into a force that he couldn't define or deny. Something attracted him.

Water trickled from portions of the surrounding walls. A spring, Thayn surmised. He moistened his fingertips and touched them to his lips. Sweet. He removed his cloak and pushed it against the water. After his cloak was clean, Thayn washed himself.

The smooth wall continued to call to him. Thayn examined it again, running his hands across it. He couldn't find a space on it unlike any other.

He scrutinized the neighboring rock. Nothing. He wasn't sure what he was looking for, but the attraction grew stronger. He must find – something – he didn't know what it was – but it was on the other side.

He ran his hands across the wall again. What was behind it? It was something that he wanted. But what? Thayn tried to dig his fingernails into the stone. Then he held a hand to his head.

Was he feeling unwell? The allure that he felt coalesced into a mood, a heavy sense of longing and loss. He ran his fingertips down the stone, then banged upon it with his fist. He turned and slid down the wall, surrendering himself to the curious depression, staring into space.

He thought about his mother and his father. He wanted to be with them again, but not as it had been.

He wanted to be with them together in a life that they hadn't shared, a memory that remembered nothing. He thought about Rykos and Ava. He wanted to sit with them again in the library at school and invent alternatives to their assignments. He thought about the Ring.

He returned to his feet and paced. He ran his fingers across every inch of the wall. He paced some more. He felt a growing presence within the stone. What was it?

Thayn put his palm to the stone. This time a crack split under his hand and ran up and down the surface. The stone pulled itself back as if a curtain to reveal a passageway. A hideous shape appeared.

"Oh." Thayn held a hand to his head. The shape changed and, vaguely familiar, slipped into the shadows. Was it – ? "Jad?"

Something caught Thayn's eye. He looked down to find a reach of bones. It rested inside on the floor to one side of the doorway.

Thayn felt a second presence. It was all around him – and then it was within him. It challenged the presence of Jad.

Voices of old women argued.

"You have no right to be here," the first presence accused, then spoke as Jad. "Come, Thayn."

"You have no right to *him*," replied the second presence. It was Jovia's voice.

"*He* found *me*." Who was this other old woman?

"*You* brought him here," Jovia objected.

"Come Thayn," Jad's voice called. Thayn felt an irresistible longing, one that could be satisfied only within the wall. "I need – "

"He's on an important journey," Jovia interrupted.

"I need him."

"No," Jovia protested.

"You no longer have power here."

"I – over you?" Jovia admitted, "No."

"Thayn?"

Thayn felt two realities. Which one of them would prevail? The presence within the wall urged him forward to join Jad. The presence within himself willed Thayn to pick up a stick of wood that lay at his feet.

Without knowing why, Thayn picked up the stick of wood. He stuck it out in front of him through the open doorway. He whispered words that he didn't understand and jumped back as, violently, the stone snapped shut.

From within the wall came a shriek of frustration. Thayn felt a breeze embrace him. He stared at the wall, dazed, flooded by confusing and conflicting thoughts.

His hand throbbed. In it he held half the stick of wood. The other half was embedded within the stone.

This wasn't Thayn's way.

CHAPTER FIFTEEN
Meeting the Master

Still dazed, Thayn stumbled away from the wall and out of the curious depression. He located a sheltered spot in a tumble of broken rock in which to rest. Immediately he fell asleep and, in troubled dreams, reviewed events of the day.

*

Thanks to Ava, Thayn's sack protected its contents well. He awoke hungry and thirsty, glad to have the provisions that she had prepared for him. Never again, Thayn decided, would he trust water that seeped from unfamiliar springs.

After a meal of hardloaf and waterfruit, Thayn returned to his previous path. The froth began to recede along its length. He slid down the shale to the basin floor. The wasteland looked even emptier and the opposite mountains farther away. Even though it would lengthen his transit, Thayn was determined to walk wide around the remaining muck. He worried what might lurk in its thickness if chalky arms reached out of its edges.

Keeping the wasteland to his side, he walked most of the morning. The sand baked underfoot. Overhead the sun blazed. Thayn pulled his cloak around him.

The bubbly crust bulged out so far that the mountains shifted, no longer rising in front of him. Instead the desert stretched until it blended with the sky. Thayn kept looking over his shoulder to keep his destination in view.

Finally the wasteland curved back on itself. The mountain leg was ahead again, much closer. It came to a soft cap halfway along its length, then descended through rolling woods to meet the basin. Thayn hastened his pace.

He was surprised when a man sprang in front of him. He was tall and the color of the sand. His eyebrows danced. "I am delighted," the man exclaimed. "So excited."

"Who are you?"

"I? You are here. I am He. I am the Master of all you see." He smiled broadly and gestured widely with both arms. One of them ended above the wrist.

Thayn tried to walk around him. In response, the Master sprang sideways. "What is this? Tell me why you think that you may pass me by."

"Why not?"

"Can it be you do not know? There is nowhere else to go." He gestured at the sand in the direction of the crusty bubbles. "Come, come and sit with me. I am the Master of all you see."

Thayn sat with the Master and looked around. To either side of him rose the mountains. The farther leg from which Thayn had traveled was rocky and inhospitable compared to the closer, more inviting slopes. In the distance, near the intersection of the two ranges, he could detect the waterfall. Between the mountains extended the wasteland along which they sat. Everywhere else was endless desert. "There isn't very much to see," Thayn noted.

"Your opinions," the Master replied quickly, "will be challenged by my minions."

He grabbed Thayn by the elbow, which Thayn didn't like, and pulled him to his feet.

Thayn pulled away. "Let go."

"Look more closely. Come along." The Master walked toward the froth and turned. "Walk this way and hear their song."

"I'm going *that* way."

The Master waved his stump.

"*We are here*," responded an eerie chorus.

"Hear them? Yes?"

Thayn cocked his head. He heard voices.

"You do. Confess."

"*And He is He,*" they sang. Again the Master smiled broadly and his eyebrows danced. Squinting, Thayn looked over the forsaken wasteland and then into it. "*He is the Master of all you see.*"

"People?" Thayn whispered.

"Yes. All of them. They are mine." He gestured with his stump. From the froth people stood at the Master's bidding, cracking the sun-bleached crust to expose a filmy world below. "Tell me, are they not divine?"

Thayn looked at them and shook his head. Slime slid from their bodies. With them came a malodorous breeze.

The Master shook his head, too. "You are right. Sad, but true. They are dull. Boring, too." He gestured at his people impatiently and several of them ducked.

He turned his attention to Thayn. "Let me take a look at you."

203

Thayn felt his arm begin to inch upward. He tried to stop himself, but couldn't. He released his cloak and it fell.

"How long has it been," the Master asked, "since I have seen such faultless skin?"

He regarded the froth, narrowing his eyes. To his minions he shouted, "You do not want to cross me, trust me. Do not watch us. You disgust me. Do not insult us with your gawking. Leave us, quickly – and no talking." The Master's minions quickly withdrew through chunks of bubbly crust.

Returning his attention to Thayn, the Master continued, "Look at you, so smooth and strong. But wait – there is something wrong. How are you alone so lucky? Why are you not foul and mucky?"

The Master attempted to probe Thayn's thoughts. "Oh." Thayn quickly blocked them.

The Master reacted with a flinch of his eyebrows. "Really now, you have powers? Yes, you do. Just like ours."

Thayn said nothing in return.

The Master ran his fingertip down Thayn's chest. "I have no love for men – or for that kind of thing. But you – you are something different – you are interesting." He ran his stump down Thayn's side.

"I sense in you a passion from forgotten days of yore." He hesitated, thinking, then continued. "But how, then, did you come here, if not through the Third Door?

"Something is amiss, something is askew – but something is exciting and inviting about you."

Thayn ran. After several steps he felt a force from behind as if he had been slapped by a great hand. He flew forward and landed face down in the sand.

"Careful," Thayn heard the Master say to himself, "do not harm him. Do not hurt him, only charm him."

In response to unspoken commands, Thayn rolled over. Involuntarily, he sat up.

"My new friend, please refrain from trying to escape again. Already now you have annoyed me." The Master approached Thayn and squatted down next to him. "Tell me, how did you avoid me?"

Thayn refused to answer. The Master continued to ramble.

"There is no other way." He looked at the near mountains and an odd expression flickered across his face. "You are not *green*. No, that is impossible, unthinkable, obscene."

The Master ran his finger down Thayn's cheek. "Look at you. What shall I do?" He rubbed his stump.

"There is something I remember from the days of old. Was it something that I saw, or something I was told?"

His eyes brightened.

"Something about trees and woods – Woods*ward*. Not about filth like you," he shouted, scolding the froth "with whom I am so bored – "

The Master raised his hand to the surface of crusty bubbles. From it a man ran forward, obviously against his will. Wearing a coat of scum, he bowed to them obsequiously, shaking. He held his arms out to the side and, as the Master prompted him, he danced until he collapsed. Others ran to retrieve him.

The Master returned to Thayn.

" – so, bored, dreary nights and days." He rubbed his stump again. "But I can learn new ways."

A thought came to Thayn as he looked at the Master's missing hand. He remembered a reach of bones. Where? He described their location aloud, "Behind the door in the mountain wall."

The Master flinched.

Thayn slowly smiled. "Yes."

The Master's expression changed, betraying fear as Thayn's smile grew. "No, I – she – "

Thayn thought quickly. "I'm her servant."

Horror seized the Master.

"I'm on her errand," Thayn added.

"To see – me?" He seemed both fearful and hopeful.

"No. An errand there." Thayn pointed below the near mountain peak. "If you continue to delay me, it'll cost you."

"Cost me what? Tell me, pray."

Thayn considered. "Another arm – and a leg."

"No," the Master conceded. "Enough. Go away."

"Offer me safe passage," Thayn demanded. He didn't like what he saw come out of the froth. Nor did he trust the Master. "And you need to answer all my questions."

The Master hesitated.

"Or I'll call her right now. You've already sensed my power."

"No, do not call her – *oh* – tell me what you want to know."

"Let's go, then," he said, getting to his feet. After walking awhile, Thayn asked, "What is this place?"

"How can you be unaware? This is the Desert of Despair."

"Have you ever been into the mountains?" Thayn asked. "Or above the falls?"

"Up there, worthless Outcasts roam. Worthy Outcasts call this home. You see, I have no affection for anything in that direction."

"The cities?"

"The cities are full of fools who make, and follow, foolish rules." Thayn and the Master reached the edge of the desert.

"I've one last question. Who lives behind the door in the mountain wall?" Thayn pointed back the way that he had come.

"Do you mean my sis – ?" The Master, realizing that Thayn was bluffing, interrupted himself. "Wait a minute, what is this – ?"

"Your sister?"

"You told me you came at her bidding," the Master objected.

"Sorry – I was only kidding." Thayn smiled at his rhyme, then explained, "I'm trying to find Vok. Have you heard of him?"

"Desist. Oh, for shame," he sputtered. "How dare you speak aloud his name?"

"He's my uncle."

Again the Master flinched and his face drained of color. "No," he cried, "oh-h." He ran to the froth and jumped headlong into it. An eruption of unseen activity cracked the crust.

*

Thayn had narrowly escaped both the Witch in the Wall and the Master of the Desert of Despair. He ran into the foothills. Compared to the opposite leg of Kala these slopes were gentle and inviting. Stands of trees thickened as Thayn ascended. He sprang into them happily. The shade felt good upon his shoulders.

As if Thayn had returned to the Ring, leaves rippled in a fragrant breeze. The trees were of a different type with bark that peeled, but their limbs were strong and broad.

Thayn climbed the soft peak that capped the summit. The view was fantastic. The far side of the mountain leg fell precipitously to meet the desert that surrounded Kala, vast and vacant.

In the direction of his intent, far along the wooded slopes, a glint of light caught Thayn's eye. Again he could see the falls that drained the lake and grasslands. He meant to travel there through the treetops.

*

The next aspect of Thayn's journey began. He worked through one great tree after another. The size of the falls, glimpses of which he caught through rustling leaves, measured his progress.

209

* Chapter Fifteen *

Thayn climbed into a tree that bloomed. Similar flowers dotted the floor below. Their fragrance was rich and heady. The next tree bloomed, too. The flowers grew increasingly beautiful as Thayn encountered more and more of them. They seemed brighter and whiter, bigger and softer, blurring in and out of focus.

Thayn continued, dreamily. Finally he reached from one tree to another and took hold of nothing. His consciousness slipped away and he fell, branch by branch, into a cluster of sweet white blossoms.

CHAPTER SIXTEEN
Yodin

Thayn awoke to familiar light that reminded him of home. A green shimmer sifted through leaves that fluttered everywhere. He did his best to look around. A wall had been cut into a hillside. Exposed roots, strong and supple, were woven into a cradle that held Thayn fast.

The world was blurry. Thayn shook his head and everything reeled. He tried to move. Not only was he bound by the cradle, but his movement sent a shiver of pain down his back and leg. "Where am I?" he asked aloud.

He heard words that he didn't understand and sensed thoughts that were meaningless. Across from him something moved in the understory, but it wasn't a bush or a tree. It was a man – of leaves?

"Oh." Thayn jerked, first in reaction to the man of

leaves, then in reaction to the pain. He forced himself to relax.

He looked around the room as best he could. Most of it was defined by the hillside. The rest was formed by heavy green trunks that reminded Thayn of the Wooden Wall. Beyond them grew greater trees, their branches forming an arching roof.

Thayn managed to free an arm. He ran his fingertips across his aching brow. "Oh." Everything seemed to fade away.

He tilted his head back, blinking, only to find another green face staring at him. It was flat with wide yellow eyes. Again he heard gibberish, but Thayn could understand this one's thoughts. "He's alive," the Green One exclaimed.

Thayn learned from his thoughts that the Green One and his companion were scouts. They protected their folk who lived in a clearing on the mountainside surrounded by idleflower. The other scout replied, but Thayn heard nothing intelligible.

But this scout – again Thayn heard the Green One think as he spoke. He poured a gray liquid from a sack into a bowl. Idleflower brew served as an antidote for the toxicity of its own perfume. "But how to make him understand?"

Thayn opened his mouth. He pointed from it to the bowl and nodded. The other scout stared, alarmed. He scratched his leafy head and said something in gibberish. Thayn heard his words aloud and, at the same time, the Green One's understanding of them. "Hold up two fingers," the Green One repeated.

Thayn did.

The other scout left abruptly.

He returned with witnesses. Green Men filled the room. They came to Thayn and spoke more gibberish, but Thayn understood none of them. Only the Green One who sat next to him made any sense. Presently he was describing the shock that he felt when Thayn had pointed to the bowl.

He offered the bowl to Thayn again. Thayn drank from it. The brew both smelled and tasted awful but immediately produced warmth that grew into his forehead. The pain in his head subsided.

The eldest among them prompted the Green One who complied, saying, "I'm Yodin. Repeat my name. Yodin."

"Yodin," Thayn responded. The Green Men murmured among themselves.

Another prompt and Yodin introduced the Old One. "This is Tadin." His leafy coat, in patches, had withered to brown and gray.

"Tadin," Thayn repeated, nodding with respect.

Tadin's singsong words made no sense, but Thayn understood Yodin's hearing of them. They asked him, "Who are you and where do you come from?"

Thayn sensed that these folk posed no threat. He wondered that he didn't know of them. Of course, the Master of the Desert of Despair had come as a surprise, too. Thayn explained, "I'm from Eator."

Obviously, the Green Men didn't understand him, either. Not even Yodin.

Thayn reached to the wall from which the roots of his cradle emerged. It was moist and his fingertip left an impression. Into the wall he scratched a map of the body of the land.

The Green Men watched him. Tadin nodded at the concept of a map. Thayn pointed to Eator. He pointed to himself and to Eator again. Then he pointed to the Green Men and to their present location as best he could figure it on the map. Thayn could feel their growing comprehension through Yodin.

"You're from the city we call," and Yodin pronounced a word that Thayn had never heard before, but he knew what Yodin meant.

Thayn nodded vigorously. Then Thayn used his

fingers to walk across the wall. He pointed to himself, then walked with his fingers some more.

Yodin guessed, "You're going somewhere?"

Thayn nodded. He made an expression that he thought would convey meaning, holding his hand to his chest and looking as if he were hungry.

"You want something?"

He nodded.

"Food?"

He shook his head. After gesturing again, Thayn walked with his fingers on the wall.

Tadin offered a suggestion.

"You want to go somewhere?" Thayn heard Yodin think.

Thayn pointed to Yutor.

There was a hush throughout the room and then more murmuring among the Green Men. Some shook their heads. Others simply stared.

Tadin cleared the room, speaking with several of the scouts before they left. Then he sat and, through Yodin, he and Thayn talked.

Thayn did his best to communicate with one hand. He was able, he hoped, to make clear that he was a Woodsward of his city.

"Seldom since the Ancient Days came to an end,"

related Tadin aloud and Yodin in thought, "have men of Kala and our folk communicated directly. We are old friends from Before Time. Since then we have become less friendly. We watch."

Tadin paused to collect his thoughts. Left to himself for a moment, Yodin was as amazed as Thayn at Tadin's words. They glanced at each other, shrugging.

Tadin studied the map. With a shriveled finger he pointed at Yutor and whispered grimly. "Evil is there," Yodin repeated in thought. Tadin made a throaty noise that didn't make sense until Thayn inferred what it was – their name for Vok.

Thayn nodded his head. He made a slashing gesture at his throat.

Tadin asked and Yodin wondered, "You mean to kill him?"

Thayn had yet to state it so plainly.

The scouts returned with white blossoms from the woods. Tadin strengthened the brew of idleflower and Thayn drank another bowl. This time warmth grew both into his forehead and down his back and leg. Within moments, all pain was gone. Again Thayn used his fingers on the wall, pointing at himself and the door until Tadin understood that he wanted to leave.

Again the Old One spoke. Yodin anticipated his

thinking. He smiled. "We have long observed Wood-swarder. Many of our ways are similar. You are in a hurry, yes, but it would be inappropriate for you to come and go without our welcome. A visit to the hot spring, a feast and some entertainment before you continue? It will fortify you for the remainder of your journey. Tadin asks me to represent our folk in honoring you."

Thayn smiled at his woody new friend. To refuse him, he reasoned, would be rude – and regrettable.

*

They traveled around the clearing of the Green Folk. It was reminiscent of the High Camp of Eator, a common area surrounded by smaller hollows. Twigs, however, appeared to be scampering about, children at play.

Broken rock appeared as they neared the spring. Steam rose from a crater of simmering water. Thayn joined Yodin in another draught of idleflower. They relaxed together.

To Thayn's delight, lithe and limber acrobats appeared. Strong and supple, they sprang into the air, balancing in unanticipated ways, swaying like treetops in the wind.

*

The next morning the Green Men prepared Thayn for the next phase of his journey. They escorted him up to a ridge that skirted the lower hip of Kala. Looking down at the swirling waterfall made Thayn feel a little dizzy.

The wasteland and desert disappeared behind him. Ahead shimmered a vast expanse of blue that seemed to have fallen from the sky, an immense lake. Beyond it the grasslands, flanked on either side by mountainous ribs, stretched to the far shoulders of the land.

Thayn and his escorts descended a steep cliff. The Green Men were careful to show Thayn the appropriate handholds and footholds. Thayn prayed to Kala for deliverance. At the base of the cliff everyone took leave of Thayn and Yodin, wishing Thayn well.

After a short hike Thayn and Yodin arrived at the water's edge. The surface of the lake broke without a splash. A figure emerged, the head of a blue man. He and Yodin spoke in similar gibberish and Thayn could hear both their thinking. Yodin asked his friend to take Thayn up the river to the Well of Understanding. The Blue One agreed.

Thayn joined the Blue One in the lake. Weedy hair floated about his face. Sleek and slippery with high shoulders and strong flanks, the Blue One pulled

Thayn down into the water and secured him into place. With a flutter of kicks and a sweep of his arms, he sliced though the water. Thayn rode him with increasing ease. They swam past a submerged city and started up the river.

*

Twirling, the Blue One skimmed the surface of the water frequently to allow himself and Thayn air. In the water the Blue One was nearly invisible. It was so that Jad and Kaden didn't see him, and only Thayn, as they passed Tordawn and the rafts.

CHAPTER SEVENTEEN
Wrack and ruin

A man in gray negotiated with the Fat One now. Kaden, Owan and Jad were released from the wall and their arms were tied behind their backs. Guards pulled the Woodswarder out of their room and prodded them along a new path. Fildor stood alone in his doorway and, when no one was looking, waved goodbye.

More men in ill-fitting gray robes waited at the ford that led from Tordawn to the interior of the land. Kaden took a quick breath at the sight of them. Both Owan and Jad glanced at him, but Kaden shook his head and looked away, his eyes narrowing.

The guards turned the Woodswarder over to the men in gray who placed them on rafts. Once across the river they were strung together again and alternated among their new captors, Jad leading the way. They began a single file into the grasslands.

None of them said a word. Jad turned, but the man behind him pushed him forward and Jad stumbled. The silence continued.

Finally, Kaden asked guardedly, "Taerl, don't you recognize me?"

None of the men in gray replied.

"Why don't you speak? Taerl?"

"Who's Taerl?" Owan whispered.

"The man in between us." Owan turned around. Taerl pushed him and Owan fell.

The men in gray stopped and the first one pulled back on Jad. Kaden stepped forward to help Owan to his feet, but Taerl restrained him.

"What's happened to you?" Kaden protested.

There was no response.

Jad was allowed to turn around now. He asked, "Who *is* he?"

Kaden remembered Taerl as a handsome man with thin features and hair lighter than his own. Now Taerl's hair was gray. His face was scarred, his nose broken and twisted. His expression was blank.

"A schoolmate. He was my neighbor prior to our Choosings. These are men of the city – men of Yutor in robes of the Ministration." Kaden's voice faltered.

Owan was on his feet again and Taerl pulled him

221

back into line. The first man pushed Jad, who turned, and they started off again.

"They won't let me turn around when we're walking – " Jad observed, pausing to check " – but they don't seem to mind if we talk as we walk."

The men in gray didn't react to Jad's assertion.

"What's wrong with them?" Owan asked.

"It's a trance, I think," Kaden replied. "The work of Vok."

"Hoo-oo-o," the men in gray howled at the sound of Vok's name.

The Woodswarder fell silent. They waited until after the agitation of the men in gray subsided. Their repeated howls notwithstanding, none fell out of step.

"So they hear us. And of – *that* name – they're aware," Jad wondered. "Of what else?"

"What do you mean?" Owan asked.

"I'm going to try something." In a menacing voice Jad threatened the men in gray, "Ha – I'm going to turn around and strike you."

No response.

He turned around and raised his fist.

He was pushed forward.

"You're uglier than you are stupid." No reaction. Jad whispered, "Vok."

"Hoo-oo-o."

"So they only hear and see – what?" Owan wondered.

"According to the will of – " Kaden stopped himself. "I won't say his name again. I don't want to hear them."

*

Kaden's city was situated within the great river's loop. A main tributary ran the length of the grassy basin through the heartland of Kala and, along with smaller streams, drained it of rain. Yutor was nestled within tall trees between the tributary and Tordawn. There were fewer rats here than on the other side of the river, but otherwise this section of the grasslands was unremarkable.

The Woodswarder and their captors walked long into the morning. The sun grew high. "Why don't we overpower them and escape?" Owan finally asked.

"Where would we run?" Jad asked in return. He noted, "We're almost to Yutor already."

"As prisoners," Owan objected.

"Perhaps it's inevitable," Kaden conceded, "upon arrival."

"What have you got in mind?"

"Nothing." Kaden lied. He was considering how

223

their entry into the Ring might play to their advantage as Woodswarder. His plans were interrupted. "Oh."

"What?" Jad and Owan asked.

Taerl was whispering. Kaden felt something touch his thoughts. He stopped short.

His plan was to surprise their captors as they entered the Ring. The change in light would affect their eyes, the Woodswarder for the better and their captors for the worse. Then he, Owan and Jad could spring into the trees.

Further attention to the details of Kaden's thinking was unnecessary. The woods toward which they made their way was notched with black. The devastation of Yutor became all too clear.

The burnt notch was a new gateway into the city. Trees, once mightiest of the Ring, were charred spires that reached up with gray and white arms, bare and broken. The light was harsh. Beyond them lay the Fallow Field.

The destruction reached out to Kaden and enveloped him. Here had been the High Camp of Yutor. It was in Kaden's sector and he had been responsible for its protection. He had failed.

They passed through the Ring and looked to either side. The pavilion was ashen. A scorch carried itself deep into the sector. Only beyond the High Camp did an inviting green resume.

There was a long rift ahead in the Wooden Wall. Crisp trunks of trees had fallen haphazardly this way and that. Their captors led the Woodswarder across the Fallow Field, a desecration. Herbs that grew upon it were trampled and bruised.

The walls along the outer paths had been smashed. Beyond them the homes of the Genexus lay in ruin. And – did Kaden believe his eyes – rats in the walkways?

The men in gray stopped outside the temple. The Woodswarder were allowed to stand together. They stared at the city. "Was this necessary?" Owan asked.

Jad shook his head, unable to reply. They looked at Kaden. His face slackened and his eyes were wells of emptiness.

To their surprise, Taerl spoke haltingly. "We're to take them to a chamber within the Center. He says to beware the tall one. The tall one means to do us violence. He senses his intent." He seemed to be listening, too.

Kaden was the tallest of the three, but his intent was shared by all.

"Who's *he*?" Owan asked.

Taerl acknowledged him now. "Vok."

"Hoo-oo-o," his companions howled. Other howls responded from within the city.

"Vok extends his best wishes." The men in gray slammed their fists into the Woodswarder's faces.

Owan fell. Jad stumbled and was struck again. Both lapsed from consciousness. Kaden remained upright. His lip split and blood trickled from it. He endured his welcome home.

The men in gray dragged Owan and Jad into the temple. Kaden walked behind them, his spirit broken. A door in the wall to the Center gaped wide. They walked through it.

All the doors of the Center were forced open. After many twists and turns they reached a small chamber and the Woodswarder were shoved inside it. Taerl unbound them and left. Other men in gray stood outside the door.

*

Revived, Owan touched Kaden's split lip with his fingertips and asked, "Does it hurt?"

"Let me be," Kaden snapped.

"Where are we?" Jad asked, rubbing a swollen eye.

"Deep within the Center of Yutor," Owan replied.

"Yes. But where are we in relation to the Hall of

Choosing?"

"Does it matter?" Owan looked puzzled.

Jad thought for a moment. "Yes, I think so."

"Why?"

Jad confessed, "I don't know."

CHAPTER EIGHTEEN
Party plans

In the High Chamber of every city of Kala, behind her respective dais, stood a High Minister, except one. In Yutor, behind the dais in the High Chamber, stood Vok. He had already summoned Taerl and paced back and forth, waiting.

At the time of his attack, Vok selected a small number of able-bodied Genexus who, spellbound, became his men in gray. Students from the school were sequestered while the majority of Yutor's population was slain. Rats that followed Vok's recruits from the grasslands discovered unanticipated bounty.

Presently doorways throughout the Center strained to shut themselves. Cracks reached out from their corners and through the surrounding stone. Outcasts and men in gray guarded the High Chamber. Its dais was cracked, too, and several portions had collapsed.

A hapless group of students knelt under the broken dais. They were unwashed and their bristlecloth tunics were torn.

The eldest among them, already a handsome young man, scrambled to his feet as Taerl entered. He was thinly featured with white blond hair. He stood up in – was it defiance? Vok studied him for a moment. No, it was an emotion that Vok didn't understand. With a thought he returned the young man to his knees.

Of Taerl he demanded, "Speak."

"We have traded well and brought you three convicts from Tordawn. They are capable of much work."

"Your thinking about them has been confusing to me," Vok complained. "You know one of them. How is this so?"

"We grew up together. He's a Woodsward of the city. The others are Woodswarder from Eator."

"Eator? How interesting. And one of them is from here? I couldn't obtain that from your thoughts." Vok considered his reflection in the dais, smiling. "You're either very weak. Or very strong."

As the twin of one and uncle of the other, Vok's resemblance to Zayn and Thayn was remarkable. His appearance was distinguished only by his cruelty. It had ravaged him, contorting his stance, creasing his

229

face and wilding his expression. His brow twitched. He grabbed several hairs that fell across his face and yanked them from his head.

At present he was tutoring the children. His pedagogy was a simple one. He brought a number of them to witness his daily business. It would train them to his purposes.

Vok's cloak wasn't made of rat skins as were the rags of his Outcast army. It was a cloak of faces sewn together. Most prominent were the High Warden and High Minister of Yutor. Other faces were chosen to be recognizable to the children. It was a component of his plan.

"So, you bring me a great prize – Woodswarder, yes. Remind me of your name."

"Taerl."

"Attention," Vok called to the children under the dais. "Listen and learn from me. This man is Taerl. He's a tool I've learned to use. As a result of his usefulness he could easily become valuable to me and, because of my expectation, he would begin to – possess me – to own me."

Vok jerked his head back and forth between the men and the children. "This will not be permitted. He must be destroyed.

"You," he gestured to the handsome young man with white blond hair. "Come to me."

The young man found his feet again.

"According to the records of this city, you've just missed your Choosing. A major event. I remember *mine* well." He smiled disingenuously. "So, a major event is due you. It will be – *of* – *my* – choosing, however. Brilliant, isn't it?

"In preparation, this man will – " Vok gestured to Taerl, looking back and forth between similar features " – oh, you know him?"

The young man sobbed, but he was brave. "He's my father."

"Really?" Vok held a hand to his mouth in mock surprise. "What a coincidence. Your name?"

"Laerl."

"I have an empty spot." Vok pointed to his cloak, then to Taerl. "Return to me, Laerl, when you have peeled from this man – his face."

"No," Laerl cried.

Vok snapped his fingers and two thick men in rat skins came forward. They pulled Laerl and his father out of the room.

The children under the dais screamed.

"Good," Vok approved, winking at them.

He returned to his place behind the broken dais. He thought out loud, as if his thinking was to be enjoyed by all. "No matter how powerful I become, fate continues to assist me. Three Woodswarder. What a spectacle this deserves."

His brow flexed uncontrollably.

"A spectacle – for the children, yes. A pageant. They'll learn so much from it.

"I'll recreate recent history – and anticipate future history. My conquest of this city – and the next – why not?

"Let me think. What will we have them – *do* – to one another?" Vok closed his eyes and smiled.

*

Kaden stood staring into space. Owan and Jad sat against a wall next to him nodding in and out of consciousness.

Thick men in rat skins burst through the doorway. They bound the Woodswarder together and pushed them out of the chamber and along numerous hallways. The Center was a maze.

Only a sampling of children visited Vok. The rest of them, spots of fading color, clung to one another in the Hall of Choosing. Jad saw them through the open doorways. Women in rat skins guarded them.

The Woodswarder were released before Vok and pushed to the floor. Vok greeted them before they regained their feet. "Welcome."

Kaden looked up at Vok. "You?" Hatred restored his spirit. He sprang toward their smiling host.

Vok held up a hand and whispered. Kaden froze in place, held by an invisible force. Vok's cloak – in horror, Kaden realized it for what it was. Some faces he remembered from his childhood, vendors from the marketplace and teachers from school whom he had known and loved. As he recognized the High Warden and High Minister, Kaden's spirit broke again, this time into pieces.

Vok wiggled his fingers. The Outcasts in the High Chamber murmured in anticipation.

The children under the dais winced.

"No," Vok resolved, jerking his head. He spoke to himself, or to those around him, it made no difference. "That would be too easy. Tempting, but it would spoil my plans. Temper, temper."

He released Kaden with a shake of his hand and Kaden fell back against Owan and Jad. "Hold him," Vok told them.

They did.

Kaden struggled.

"No," Jad cautioned Kaden.

"How brave you are," Vok commended Jad. "You have courage to tell him 'no.' He's obviously your superior. Or do you tell him 'no' to please me?"

Jad frowned.

"I didn't think so." Vok stared at them. One by one, the Woodswarder looked away. Finally Vok decided, "You're *boring*."

Two Outcasts snorted. Vok pointed at them. He had learned a game from the Master in the Desert of Despair.

"Ha," laughed the first Outcast again.

"Ha, ha," returned the other, stepping forward.

They continued laughing, face to face.

"Ha."

"Ha, ha."

Vok twirled a finger. They circled each other.

"Ha, ha, *ha*."

"Ha, *ha*, ha, ha."

They sprang and fell. Their laughter grew louder as they rolled over each other. The first Outcast took hold of his opponent's head and slammed it against the floor. The other slashed out at him, using his hands as claws. They sought each other's throat, gasping for breath.

Their laughter grew higher in pitch and quicker in pace until, abruptly, it stopped. Their heads fell at odd angles. The throat of the first Outcast was slashed and the neck of the other was broken.

The children cried.

"*That* was *not* boring." Vok stared again at the Woodswarder. "That was fun. And oh, what fun the four of us shall have, my new friends. And fun for the children."

Kaden glanced at the little ones under the dais.

Vok continued knowingly, "You are from Yutor, of course. I can sense your loyalty and concern.

"Do you know what I think of your children?" He looked from Owan to Jad and Kaden. A slow change of expression tugged at Vok's face. "No, I mean *my* children, don't I? You don't have children. You have other interests."

Then Vok shouted furiously, "I think your children are soft. Soft and shallow. Insubstantial. They're in desperate need of hardening – *if* they're to be of any use to me at all. Otherwise, they're dead.

"And you, my new friends, will be both. Useful to me, and – well, I'm getting ahead of myself.

"We'll recreate for the children my latest glory. A pageant. You – " he pointed to Kaden " – will be the

235

High Warden.

"You – " he pointed to Owan " – oh, I don't care about you."

He pointed to Jad. "You will run away – like *you* did." He pointed to Kaden again.

Kaden glared at him, his expression hot and icy.

Vok frowned. "You don't expect a repeat performance, do you? A second chance?

"But – " he spoke to Jad " – you'll come running back again, won't you?"

Again Kaden took a step toward Vok.

"No." Jad's warning came too late. Again Vok immobilized Kaden.

"That's the most important part," Vok explained. "Running back again. Making the same mistakes. Important to *me*.

"Perpetuity," he breathed. "I may need it more later than I need it now." He chuckled to himself.

"Now, let's get down to details, shall we? The children will sit in the audience. The three of you will stand there and be Woodswarder of Yutor and do – whatever it is you do – *protect*, I suppose – " he rolled his eyes " – and then –

" – but – what's this?" Vok stopped. Again he smiled disingenuously. He closed his eyes and held his hands to his temples. "Impossible."

Vok swept back around the dais. He walked along it, clutching his head. "No," he shouted. He brought down his fist. Another portion of the dais collapsed.

"Return them," he called to the thick men, releasing Kaden from his spell. "Take them all away and leave me be. I must think. Go."

The thick men pushed the children and Woodswarder out of the High Chamber. They heard more shouting and another splitting of stone.

CHAPTER NINETEEN
The Diversionary

Thayn rode the Blue One upriver. They passed under the rafts that ferried Kaden, Jad and Owan to the island city of Tordawn. Thayn didn't notice them. The sky and the water mingled together into a fluid blue. Thayn lost his sense of time and place.

The current quickened as the land rose. The river curved. Bubbles eddied in all directions and sunlight played among them.

Morning grew into afternoon. The river doubled back on itself and, as the day progressed, the sun seemed to return to its previous position. They passed another island and the ruin of Tordusk, abandoned even by Outcasts.

They continued in the shadow of the ribbed highlands opposite Eator. As the high hip of Kala grew nearer, the river narrowed and deepened. Its banks changed from grass to rock.

Evening settled over the land. The river squeezed under an arch of stone to become the glassy pool of a grotto. Water trickled from a tunnel in its far wall. The Blue One swam to the far side of the pool and rolled headlong. Thayn slipped onto a smooth stony edge and rolled over.

Thayn realized where he was according to the map of the land that he often drew. Beneath rounded peaks a spur of the mountains reached into the grasslands. The grotto rested within it.

The Blue One brought him food, a type of stalk that Thayn had never seen. Soon his sack was stuffed with them. "Thank you." Thayn thought that he saw others in the water, but he couldn't sense them.

"Your thoughts are turbulent," noted the Blue One. "They are troubled, as if water afraid to fall. They swirl, but shape themselves around nothing."

Thayn found the Blue One's thinking difficult to understand. "Where would they fall?" Thayn asked.

"Into the Well of Understanding, if you let them. Your thoughts are too agitated. Let me relieve you of them."

"No – thanks. I wish it were that easy. I need to remember everything I know." Thayn was protecting

Jovia's teachings.

"Why?"

"There's so much I need to figure out."

"What?"

"My way to Yutor, I guess, but that's just part of it. It's a puzzle I need to put together."

"How? You are but one piece."

Thayn sighed. "I have to try."

"You must try harder." The Blue One arched into the air and disappeared into the water without a ripple. Thayn watched the still surface of the pool. Was the Blue One really gone?

Thayn sat for a moment to catch his breath. He thought about all that was happening to him. Nothing fit together. He looked at the pool and out through the arch of stone. Framed by broken boulders, the grasslands reached to the sky.

The Well of Understanding? What was it? Where was it? Thayn was weary of puzzles. He closed his eyes. He saw black, then white.

What would he do? Where would he go? Thayn squinted. White turned to yellow and he grew afraid. Then yellow turned to red and anger. Thayn grew angry at Kala.

He opened his eyes again, turned the other way and

looked up the tunnel. A rivulet traveled along its floor. The tunnel curved and continued out of view, its walls tinged pink.

The choice was easy. Thayn wouldn't go back the way that he had come. He started up the tunnel. As long as there was a direction in which to go, he decided, it was the right one.

The last time that he made a similar decision it led Thayn to the Desert of Despair. Where would it lead him now?

The tunnel glowed faintly, dim but never dark. Its pink walls deepened in color. After a curve it split into two smaller tunnels. Thayn chose one of them without thinking.

He stopped. Did something call him? He went back and looked along the other way. Both tunnels appeared identical. Which one of them was right?

With a shrug, Thayn continued. Again he came to a fork. This time one of the smaller tunnels ascended and the other one descended. Along both of them a rivulet continued, flowing down one and, to Thayn's amazement, up the other. He followed his curiosity and stepped carefully down the slick slope. Water splashed up against his toes.

The tunnel opened again, branching up and down

and sideways, and along every floor a trickle of water flowed. After a precarious hop, Thayn continued sideways for awhile.

He felt both a sense of resolve – he had to keep going, it was the only way – and a sense of futility – surely there were too many choices and he would make a wrong turn.

Without warning, the tunnel opened into a great cavern. It was spherical, and through it in all directions extended pillars of palest pink. Everywhere were openings as the one in which he stood, other tunnels, and in every one of them Thayn saw himself. In some doorways he stood sideways, in others he stood upside down or at that angle or this.

Thayn took a step forward and all the openings except the one in which he stood disappeared. Everything became level again. Pink pillars of smooth stone reached between arched ceilings and the floor.

Two broad domes opened into each other as they curved together. Thayn walked to the middle of one of them. Here several pillars rested on their sides, defining an inner circle from which a center column rose. A similar column stood in the middle of the other dome.

Thayn had been in the company of others for so long that he expected someone to appear and greet him. He waited. No one came.

He explored the caverns. Their symmetry was almost perfect – every counterpoint looked the same, but one was missing. There was no other opening except the one through which he arrived.

Conflicting thoughts and feelings returned to him. Thayn was glad to be alone. He was tired of others' expectations. Perhaps now he could make sense out of things. Perhaps he could puzzle things together.

But why was he here? Who would direct him on his way?

Thayn circled the domes several times. He looked into every recess and behind every pillar. He found nothing. He touched the walls. There was no response. The stone was smooth and warm.

He returned to the ring of fallen pillars and sat on one of them. Adding to Thayn's confusion was a feeling of excitement that he couldn't deny. It seemed to come through the floor, the walls. It permeated the place. Thayn ran a hand over his face and down his chest. He looked at the standing center column. Water ran both up and down it.

He watched the flowing water for a moment. He grew impatient and walked around the cavern again. Was there really no other way out?

Thayn stopped at the other ring and sat. Again he grew angry. Thoughts flickered through his head like forgotten coals that fanned into flame. He thought of his father. He could still see Zayn's wild expression dissolve into a bland mask as his mind closed. He thought of Jovia, whom he had always blamed, and of Vok, whom he hadn't known to blame. He knew *now*. And now was he, a victim of all that happened around him, expected to save and protect others little worse off than himself? Why? It wasn't fair.

Thayn stood and paced a little. He felt as if he'd eaten too many berries, but he'd eaten nothing. Perhaps he should. He went back to the other stone ring, sat and opened his sack. No, he wasn't hungry.

He was tired of his anger and frustration, and of captivity. He stared into space, refocusing on the far center column.

There was a palpable beauty to the place. Thayn took a deep breath and it calmed him. How long since he had attended to his own needs? Too long. "That's for sure," he whispered to himself. It felt good to grasp something that was undeniable. Thayn resolved, from that moment on, to be truer to himself.

He decided to go back the way that he had come after all. He returned to – where was it? The opening in the wall? "No." He couldn't find it.

He slipped into a mood that he hadn't experienced since he stood under a moon that looked out of place in the afternoon sky. Thayn remembered longing for something that didn't yet make sense. So much had happened since then. Did things make more sense now? No, they were worse than ever. But the longing that he felt had been satisfied between then and now. Thayn didn't realize it until he felt it again.

What was it? What had he lost? What didn't he know he had? It was a sense of fulfillment. Yes. Of completion.

Jad – of course.

In the company of Jad, all had been enough. In Jad's eyes, Thayn saw the world as he wanted it to be.

*

Ava sat alone in the Center. Whatever would become of her? And Rykos? He remained at home with Aryla's aunt and uncle. They baked while Aryla and her mother spent long days behind the counter of their booth in the marketplace. Rykos shook his head at the unfortunate turn in events. Ava sighed.

Both of them had been relieved by Elyda of their duties and relegated to their quarters since they were discovered in the Hall of Choosing. They both knew that their punishment was mild compared to the High Minister's displeasure. Elyda didn't want anyone to know of their crime. She told Cyrll that she had sent Thayn to join Kaden's party.

Rykos and Ava were careful. They did nothing to call further attention to themselves. Elyda was acting in peculiar ways. They worried that she was unwittingly affected by Vok.

Ava hadn't taken from Rykos the powers that she had given him. Their discovery in the Hall of Choosing had been too abrupt for her to do so. They should have worn off by now, but for reasons that neither of them understood, Rykos' powers had grown stronger.

Demands were too much for Elyda. She denied what she couldn't control. Rykos' awareness of her instability was enough to make clear that something was terribly wrong. As a Ministrant, Ava's ability to visit Elyda's thoughts wasn't uncommon, although Ministration always selected carefully what to share. Rykos' access to Elyda was without precedent.

Clumsy with his powers, Rykos failed to hide them well. Perhaps it was good that he wasn't allowed to leave home. As he heard Aryla's thoughts he anticipated her words, fulfilling her wishes before she shared them. "Just like Father. It's as if you could read my mind," she said to him.

In order to shield the city from curiosity about Rykos and Ava, Elyda told others that, due to their talents, they had been chosen to do special work for the Center. Countless notebooks were brought to them for review, but they were blank.

*

All were prisoners. Kaden, Owan and Jad remained under heavy guard in Yutor. Thayn sat in the pink cavern, and Ava and Rykos in their quarters.

PART FOUR

CHAPTER TWENTY
Lessons

"Something must be done."

"Yes."

"It's time. It's time."

Rykos, Ava and Thayn heard voices.

*

Rykos heard them in the kitchen. He went to the doorway. "There you are. Let me look at you. Are you treating my daughter well?"

"Boz?"

"Come and sit with me. We need to talk."

*

Ava closed her eyes and concentrated. She recognized two of the voices. One of them belonged to Boz. And, when she opened her eyes, the owner of the other voice that she recognized stood in front of her.

"Jovia?"

"There's more I must share with you, my child. There's much more we must do."

*

Thayn spun around at the sound of the voices. Was he dreaming? No, he was wide awake. "Let's begin."

An old man appeared out of nowhere. "Lor?"

"Tell me all you've learned since I saw you last."

"What?"

"Tell me everything I don't know."

"Lor, I'm so glad to see you." Thayn meant to embrace him.

"I'm aware of that." Lor stepped away, but a smile flitted across his face at Thayn's intentions. "Don't blather. Time is short. Tell me."

"Tell you what?"

"Everything."

"Since you've been gone? Let me see. Jovia's gone, too. She died – "

"Of Jovia I know. I'll take you to her."

"You will?"

"Continue."

"Vok – "

"Of Vok I know. Continue."

"Kaden – "

"Yes?"

"He's leading a mission to Yutor."

"I know. Continue."

"What *don't* you know?" Thayn asked.

"I don't know what you don't know. Why are you here?"

As was so often the case, Thayn wasn't exactly sure what Lor meant. "Philosophically, you mean?"

"No, here in this place."

"Oh – I can't find my way out."

"Where are you going?" Lor inquired. "Who told you to come here?"

"Yutor. Yodin. Or was it the Blue One?"

"You are on a mission. Why have you abandoned it?"

"He told me I can't solve the puzzle."

"Why?"

"I'm only a piece."

"Let us start over again. Why did you begin this journey?"

"You came to me in a dream, remember?" Thayn rubbed his forearm as he thought. "You, Jovia and Boz. Then Ava and I opened the Third Door."

"Why?"

Thayn frowned. "I was going to ask *you*."

"Look what you're doing. Tell me, why are you doing that?"

"Rubbing my arm? I don't know. It didn't break. Yes, that's why. The breaking of arms. It must be stopped."

"Why?"

"Or it will continue."

"The breaking of arms? All of them?"

"What funny questions you ask. Yes – " Thayn thought for a moment " – no. Just the next one. The next opportunity."

"And what would that involve?"

"The children of Yutor?"

"Yutor is already broken."

Thayn's eyes grew wide. "Eator? Kaden will call Vok's attention to Eator again. A continuation of violence, like the breaking of arms. Eator will be next."

Lor nodded. "What must be done?"

"The chain needs to be broken."

"How many links?" Lor asked.

"All of them – no, just one," Thayn realized. "The next one."

"So?"

"So a single piece *is* the whole puzzle."

"I have taught you well. Tell me again, why are

you here?"

"Yodin asked the Blue One to bring me here. I'm on my way to Yutor."

"What have you found here?" Lor asked.

"Not the Well of Understanding."

"You sense nothing?"

"Not really. Only – " Thayn hesitated.

"Only what?"

"Something I forgot, maybe. Or I didn't know I had it. Now it's no better than a memory."

"And it's this memory you follow?"

"I'm trying to follow Kaden's party – to protect them – to prevent Kaden from the part he's playing in the – what we just talked about – the *perpetuity* of Vok. Is that what you want me to say?"

"Is it true?"

"You're confusing me."

"Tell me, is that what you follow?" Lor's voice grew shrill.

"No."

"What, then, or who?"

"Jad," Thayn concluded at last.

"Yes."

Thayn thought for a moment. He repeated Lor's question. "So why did the Blue One bring me here?"

"Let me suggest two reasons," Lor replied. "One involves you and the other involves us all. You stand in the Diversionary. Don't you feel it? It may be more diverting as you learn how to use it. The other reason is because you are near the Well of Understanding."

"This isn't the Well – ?"

"No."

"It isn't? But there's nowhere else to go," Thayn protested, "except back the way I came. And I can't find it anymore."

"What lies that way?"

"A tunnel. A pool. And beyond it the river and the land."

"What else did the Blue One say to you?"

"I need to release my thoughts – because they're turbulent, too agitated or something. It doesn't make sense."

"Perhaps that's why you came here first. It will clear your thinking," Lor said.

"What will?"

Lor disappeared.

"Wait – " Lor was already gone. Thayn walked to the rock ring and sat. He tried to collect his thoughts, but Lor's visit had scattered most of them. One prevailed – namely, it was Jad's companionship that he sought. In time, it was the only thought that remained.

"Would it help to remember your purpose?" a familiar voice asked. From the center column stepped a vague shape. It defined itself.

"Jad?"

*

No further words were needed in the Diversionary. Jad and he were of a like mind and a single purpose – Thayn's purpose. He felt nothing but the unification in which he and Jad existed.

Later Thayn opened his eyes. Jad stepped from the column, a fresh smile on his face. Thayn laughed as events repeated themselves. "Wait a minute. Let's talk. Tell me about your mission."

"That's not my purpose here. I know only as you inform me."

"As I – ?" Thayn realized what was happening. This wasn't Jad. He was an illusion.

*

Countless times the illusion reappeared. Jad lay along a fallen pillar now. He reached out his hands to Thayn.

"Come," Jad invited.

But it wasn't Jad, not really. He was as Thayn "informed" him – wasn't that what the illusion had said?

Thayn was conflicted. He was angry that Jad was an illusion, but happy that the illusion was Jad.

Countless times Thayn's anger lost out. Again, the moment prevailed. Everything was right.

"But here in the Diversionary, Jad is nothing more than this." Thayn bent over and kissed the illusion of Jad a last time. Heartened, he resolved to continue his journey. "I have to go."

*

Thayn's way appeared again. He returned through the tunnel. It no longer branched at every opportunity, but sloped gently down to the grotto. The Blue One waited.

"You're back. Good. Join me." Thayn entered the still pool, treading water as best he could. Weedy blue hair floated about the Blue One's face. "Your thoughts have acquired ballast."

"Where is the Well of Understanding?"

"I can only lead you to it. You must allow yourself to enter. Be strong. The need grows."

Only because it suddenly made sense, Thayn held his arms over his head and pointed his feet. He sank quickly.

The pool was throated deeply like the blue flowers that, among thickets of scrub, fringed the Ring. Thayn was gliding sideways within a curving funnel of stone. The water was warm and heavy and, during his transit, Thayn felt no need for breath.

After countless twists and turns the rock opened overhead. Thayn found himself in the depths of a new pool. He righted himself, pushed against its floor and rose up through the water, breaking the surface.

This pool sat in a cavern of iridescent white stone. Its walls weren't smooth as those in the Diversionary. Instead, they were sharp and jagged.

Whisperings flew over his head. The air was thick with prayer. Vaults of faceted crystal pulsed with light that burst free to meet approaching praise and supplication. This was a temple.

Openings in the temple wall led to an isolated bluff surrounded by sand. It was the same desert into which Kala fell. Several similar bluffs reached to the main body of the land, its mighty shoulders growing to either side.

Why was Thayn here? Certainly he was no closer to Yutor. His exploration of the temple was hindered by its design. Most of its ministry involved rarefied thoughts and there were few pathways among the crystals for pedestrian thinking. Ducking to avoid incoming prayer, Thayn stared up into the inaccessible archways that glimmered with hope and sparkled in celebration.

Thayn wanted to be up there. He tried to climb several crystals but their sides were too slippery. What would he do now? He fought away anger that, even in this place, found him.

Of course. There was a simple solution. Thayn prayed. He felt his spirit leap into the air and sail high overhead. His prayer returned ablaze with light that landed atop a nearby crystal. It would serve as a dais. Thayn looked into the stone and an old woman looked back. Gray hair escaped her wimple.

"Jovia?"

"You've come," she said. "Good."

"Is it really you? What are you doing here?"

"I'm a steward of the temple. We've little time. Are you ready?"

"I guess so – for what?"

"Below is a puzzle."

Thayn looked down. At his feet lay broken tablets.

"Place them on the dais, upside down," Jovia instructed. "They will make more sense to you if you don't try to read them. Look only at their shape."

Thayn did as he was told. The tablets had been smashed into pieces, but their shapes were distinctive.

He repositioned the pieces into place. Soon the tablets were intact again.

"I can read them," Jovia shared from within the crystal. "This is good. Turn the pieces over and transpose them right side up, so you may study them, too."

Again Thayn did as she said. He reassembled the tablets. As his eyes met the words, he could hear Jovia recite them.

"But I don't know what any of this means," Thayn complained.

"It will make sense to you as you need it. That's the nature of truth. For instance, look to the side of the dais."

Thayn found nothing but a withered bush. Several phrases from the tablets came into his thoughts. He repeated them aloud.

The branches of the bush quivered. They reached into the air, burst into blossom and bore fruit. These were berries of colors that Thayn had never seen.

"Eat one," Jovia directed him.

Thayn plucked a speckled berry and held it to his lips. He bit into it.

*

It was at this moment that Vok hesitated in describing his plans to the Woodswarder. "What's this?"

he asked. He perceived the power of the berry before Thayn himself sensed it.

Then Vok was smashing his fist against the dais of Yutor.

*

Thayn stood looking into the crystal again. Jovia's face faded. Thayn thought of her as he last saw her alive. Words came to him and he whispered them. Instantaneously he was with her in the Forbidden Room. "Practice," Jovia encouraged him.

Thayn thought of home, first as a Woodsward in the Ring. He whispered again and the pavilion appeared. He saw Cyrll and his captains. They sat exactly as Thayn remembered them, but obviously they didn't see him.

Thayn thought about his family. They sat around the table at dinner engaged in conversation, all except his father, who stared at him. He blinked. This wasn't a memory. These thoughts occurred in the present.

"Careful," Jovia cautioned him. Thayn didn't remain there.

With Jovia's guidance Thayn sorted out his new powers. He learned the difference between revisiting a memory and transporting himself somewhere in real time. The words were different and came to him with

259

his intent. He learned to be careful with his thoughts and, more particularly, with his wishes.

More than once, images of Jad flickered across the dais. Thayn remembered him standing within the truncated tree in the Ring of Eator. He watched Jad as he sat imprisoned in Yutor.

Jovia wouldn't release Thayn from her tutelage until he had proven mastery of his new powers. "Soon you won't rely on the dais. The berries will be enough and, in time, they won't be necessary, either. Powers will come to you in response to need. But you must work very hard."

For the present Jovia let Thayn rest. All too soon their task would resume. Thayn lay down, exhausted, and immediately he fell asleep.

*

Jovia had one last errand. She found Ava and whispered in her ear, "Go to him."

Ava followed Jovia's thinking and it led her to Thayn. His mind was open to her. She sorted through his thoughts and discovered many useful things.

CHAPTER TWENTY-ONE
Child's play

Returned to their chamber in the Center of Yutor and guarded by men in gray, the Woodswarder reacted to their situation in different ways. Jad's primary concern was for the children. "What do we do now?"

Kaden wavered between purpose and despair. He wondered, "Does it matter?"

Owan considered their own welfare. "It matters to *us*." He and Jad collaborated on a plan.

*

"Oh-h-h," the Woodswarder bellowed. They lay on the floor and clutched their bellies.

The men in gray came to see why they cried. The Woodswarder sprang to their feet. Owan and Jad each grabbed a guard by the throat and Kaden dispatched them with a quick fist.

"Let's go." The Woodswarder raced through the

Center. Nobody in the city had a thought of his own.
Speed and surprise were to their advantage. Before the
news of their escape reached Vok, the Woodswarder
were sprinting along the Great Path past the auditorium. It was shattered.

They entered the school. It, too, lay in ruins. "I
have an idea. This way," Owan directed them.

"Where are you – ?" Kaden asked.

Owan interrupted him, "If your city is designed the
same as – I wonder – yes – here." Jad and Kaden followed him into the offices.

"Owan – ?"

"I was never a very good student. I used to talk
too much – at least that's what they told me. They put
me in detention all the time – in here."

They entered a small room adjoining the offices.
Owan slid a stone plate off an opening in the floor and
dropped into a recess. Jad asked, "A service shaft?"

Owan smiled. "I used to go all over Eator during
detention. When my time was up, I came back."

Jad glanced at Kaden and they shrugged. With res-
ignation – and some trepidation – they joined Owan.
He slid the stone back into place over their heads.

"Do you really think this is safe?" Jad asked.

"They never caught me," Owan added.

"I'm sure Vok will find us, given time." Kaden's eyes narrowed. "This may be enough to throw him off track for awhile."

"Perhaps we should find him first. We could surprise him," Owan proposed.

"Do these shafts lead into the Center?"

"They lead everywhere."

"Maybe there's still something to eat in the kitchens."

"Or the marketplace."

"Let's go see."

*

Vok stood motionless behind the broken dais. Few portions of it remained intact. All his energy went into sensing Thayn. He felt Thayn's powers ripen. Thayn visited his memories and different places throughout the land. Vok even sensed him several times within Yutor itself.

Thayn lingered in no place for more than moments and it took all Vok's concentration to stay abreast of him. If only he stayed somewhere long enough, Vok would go to him.

He wouldn't confront Thayn in the temple of Kala. There Vok wouldn't prevail.

*

When Thayn rested, Vok returned to himself. He discovered that the Woodswarder had escaped. Furious, he tried to locate them. He was unaware of the service shafts, however, and his thoughts reached into ways that made no sense.

*

The Woodswarder's guards were taken to the High Chamber. A clutch of children continued to sit among the rubble under the dais. Vok revived the guards. In response to his will and whimsy they punished each other until they welcomed death. The older children opened their arms to the younger ones and shielded their eyes.

"How sweet," Vok observed. "A natural tendency to protect the young, of course. It suggests more appropriate players for my pageant."

He planned out loud again.

"Why should I arrange for violence among the Woodswarder with children in the audience – ?" he regarded the innocents huddling under the dais " – when it can just as easily be the other way around?

"Besides, there are so many of them. I don't want *all* of them. Come to think of it, I don't want *children*. What was I thinking? I need only the older ones to serve me and perpetuate my power. Why should I take the time to teach them all and wait, wait, wait? I'll have that much less to do. Brilliant."

He called to the thick men. "Take them. And get rid of those two," he added, pointing to the unfortunate guards.

"I feel better," Vok admitted to himself. "Still, I need to think. I must be careful."

*

The children told the others in the Hall of Choosing what they had learned. Some of them started crying. Women in rat skins threatened to throw them through the Third Door if they didn't stop.

Many of the children no longer sought comfort. They hardened according to Vok's plan. Imagining violence among themselves, they grew suspicious of one another.

*

Kaden, Owan and Jad heard the children's cries through the shafts under the city. They were distant, but unmistakable. With only a shared nod the Woodswarder went in search of them.

The children's cries, after many turns and retracing of steps, were almost overhead. Owan hunted the surrounding shafts for an exit but couldn't find one.

*

Vok made final plans for his pageant. He'd have to find another venue. There wasn't enough room in the High Chamber for everyone to participate.

The auditorium was so large and impersonal. Vok wanted a more intimate setting. He, too, wondered if this city was arranged as his was. If so, a little lecture hall joined the Center to the school.

He made his way through the halls and gaping doorways to find it. "Yes. This will do nicely."

*

Vok returned to the High Chamber. Laerl waited for him. He held between his forefingers and thumbs his father's face.

"There's a good boy," Vok praised him. With it, his cloak was complete.

*

Thayn stirred. He heard someone call his name. "Thayn." It took him a moment to figure out where he was. He had been so many places recently and had heard so many voices. He rubbed his eyes and brushed the hair off his brow.

The temple of Kala came into focus. "Thayn?" Jovia called again. He got to his feet. Jovia looked out of the crystal at him.

"Yes?"

"We need to continue."

"I'm so tired. I need to sleep."

"He won't come here. You must busy him – keep him distracted. It will buy us time. Otherwise, he may strike before we're ready."

"Ready for what?"

*

Boz visited Rykos for a last time. Rykos was frustrated. "If I have this – power – and all this responsibility, as you remind me, why do I need to sit here and do nothing?"

"Some people go to their purpose. Others, their purpose comes to them. They need to be ready for it. It's no better, one way or the other. Both ways work – *when* they work.

"In your case, Rykos – in our case – " Boz continued " – part of our 'power' comes from its unsuspected source. In other words, part of our power is that few would suspect us of having it. That's why you have to sit here and do nothing until it's time to do something. When you are needed, you will be sought. Then you'll remember your restlessness as you kiss your wife and unborn baby goodbye and risk everything you treasure."

"Baby?"

*

Chapter Twenty-one

"Come," Thayn taunted, "and get me, Vok."

"No, he's on me again." Vok moaned. He held his hands to his head. His Outcast army and men in gray didn't know how to respond to his outbursts. They did nothing as Vok's interludes of madness preoccupied him.

Between delusional episodes Vok was the same as ever. He planned his spectacle involving the children. He never questioned its success.

Then, "He's on me again."

Previously it was Jovia who uttered these words and "he" was Vok. Now they were Vok's words and "he" was Thayn. Jovia taught Thayn how to insinuate himself into Vok's mind and plague his thoughts. The temple of Kala intensified Thayn's power to irresistible proportion.

Although Thayn learned quickly, the expense of energy exhausted him. Jovia concentrated on keeping him conscious but, before long, it was impossible. He slumped against the crystal dais and wouldn't rouse.

Vok renewed himself as Thayn slept.

*

Arrangements were finally complete. "Bring the children." Thick men in rat skins prodded the children out of the Hall of Choosing and herded them to the back of the school. They cried.

Below them, the Woodswarder followed. They hurried through the service shafts until the children were almost overhead. This time Owan found an exit. A stone plate in a corner of the lecture hall covered an opening in the floor. The Woodswarder waited beneath it.

Vok sensed them now. No other concerns distracted him. "Ladies and gentlemen, welcome to my show." He directed a meager audience of Outcasts to their seats.

Reaching in thought among the children, he found the two who were most afraid. "Come." They sobbed their way to the front of the stage, two ragged moppets. Spellbound, they prepared to fight each other.

"But it seems a shame there are so few of you to witness this," Vok interrupted. He scowled in concentration. The stone plate in the corner slid across the floor. Through the opening, suspended by Vok's will, Kaden, Owan and Jad were lifted into the room.

*

"Thayn. You must awake."

Thayn pulled himself to his feet. He looked into the dais. Jovia showed him the events in Yutor as they occurred in real time. Thayn selected a dappled berry according to his newly acquired senses. It was tangy. He whispered words from the tablets. His thoughts burst and he felt himself fly through them.

*

The Woodswarder stood facing Vok. Beside himself, seemingly, Vok appeared again. Kaden flinched. Owan rubbed his eyes. Jad exclaimed, "Thayn – ?"

"Jad, run."

Vok whirled his head, looking from Thayn to Jad and back again. "Excellent. Thank you."

Thayn braced himself, fortifying his mind against Vok's attack. It wasn't necessary. Vok directed his attention elsewhere. Without warning, Jad flew across the room. With a thud, he slammed against the wall. "Thayn – ?" He fell to the floor.

"Jad – " Thayn cried " – no."

Vok laughed. "Child's play."

Shakily, Jad stood. "Oh-h." He sailed back the other way, hit the opposite wall and fell again.

This time he didn't get up.

Thayn ran to him. "Jad?"

*

In the audience frightened eyes looked up at two strangers who appeared out of nowhere. The strangers immediately fell to their knees. Dressed in faded rags, they blended in with the children.

One of the children asked the strangers, "Who are you?"

In response, Rykos held a finger to his lips.

"Hush," Ava whispered.

CHAPTER TWENTY-TWO
Drama extempore

"What have we here?" Vok asked, looking at a younger version of himself unblemished by the ravages of cruelty. "A tableau? How touching." Thayn knelt on the floor, Jad in a heap before him.

"Don't try," Vok commanded over his shoulder. Kaden and Owan had started toward Vok, but they flew back through the air.

"Oh-h." They, too, lay limp on the floor.

Thayn glared at Vok.

Vok smiled in return. "High time you got here – although not as I hoped. You're as stubborn as – but I digress. Alak – how handsome you are. Everyone, I'd like you to meet my nephew. Do you see the family resemblance?" Vok jerked his head in the direction of the audience and emptied his mind of thought. His expression slackened and softened.

Kaden stared up at him. No wonder he had confused uncle with father and son. Undefined by their
personalities, they were nearly identical.

Vok refilled his mind and his thoughts disfigured
him. "So what to do now? Back to my original idea, I
think. I've the right to change my mind, haven't I?"

There was no response.

Vok looked at the children and rolled his eyes.
"So poorly trained. Let's try it again.

"I've the right to change my mind, haven't I?" He
waved his hand at them.

"Yes," came their involuntary chorus.

"Much better. So, on with our business. Our little
show. You didn't think you were going to appear out
of nowhere and save the day, did you, nephew? How
trite that would be. It's not part of the plot. Or perhaps
I wax extempore. Who would know?"

He glanced around the room expectantly. Nobody
returned a comprehending look.

"Perhaps it's just as well." Vok continued, softly
but loud enough to be heard by all. He paused between
words as if to stretch their importance. "You see I'm
not – really an actor – at heart. I'm – pretending. But
life is stranger than fiction, and now we have someone
who can – play – my part – in this enterprise. I'll join

the children in the audience."

To Thayn he feigned and fawned, "I'm already an ardent admirer."

Vok pointed a finger at Jad who immediately re-vived. Kaden and Owan, unsteady, were already on their feet. "To your places, everyone."

The Outcasts quieted the children. The children's thoughts were disorderly and Vok didn't bother to review them. He didn't sense two among them who didn't belong.

*

Not only had his party plans and Thayn's frequent visits preoccupied Vok, they distracted him from Ava's recent activities. She had been busy. Jovia's last visit led her to Thayn. His mind was open to her and she acquired from him the power of transportation.

Undetected by Vok, Ava visited Yutor. Through Jad she learned of the children's location, welfare and appearance. She and Jovia considered a novel strategy. "Never send a man to do a child's job." All was ready.

In Eator, Ava summoned Rykos. She handed him faded leggings and a ragged tunic. "Ava?"

"Change into these."

Rykos did as he was told.

"Now take my hand." They appeared in Yutor and

hid among the children. Ava emptied her and Rykos'
minds and they waited.

*

"It seems a shame to rush things so." Vok directed
his pageant from the audience. "There are so many op-
tions. Perhaps some opening entertainment, yes. A
little exposition. *Ahem.*

"This is a story of Woodswarder." Vok returned to
the stage. "Woodswarder are – now how would we describe them? What does one think of when one thinks
of Woodswarder?"

The Outcasts in the audience murmured.

"I know – but we can't do that *here*." Vok looked
around the lecture hall. His eyes came to rest on a side
door. "Of course."

Vok selected from the audience his favorite, the
handsome young man with white blond hair. "Come."
Laerl obeyed. Vok clutched him by the throat.

"*Protect,* yes," Vok remembered. Excitedly, he
asked the Woodswarder, "You'll want to protect him,
won't you? It will require your cooperation."

He waved his free hand at the children, rendering
them deaf. "Rest your ears, little ones, until we get to
the important part of the story. We wouldn't want
them to hear," he told the Woodswarder.

275

"That way." He indicated a side door to the stage and squeezed Laerl's throat. "You wouldn't want me to hurt him."

Laerl groaned, "Oh."

"That way," Vok repeated, following the Woods-warder.

The side door led to a small preparation room. It held only a couple of tables. "As I was saying, how would we describe Woodswarder – on a typical day? Hmm...

"What do you think, Laerl? But of course, you don't really know, do you? But who among us hasn't heard rumors?

"You know, of course, they're strong. And brave. And unusually attractive, aren't they? To *each other*."

"Vok, no," Kaden protested.

"And virtuous. So repugnantly virtuous. You revolt me." He spat in Kaden's face.

"Oh," Laerl groaned again as Vok tightened the grip on his throat.

"And intrigue me." He licked his spittle from Kaden's cheek.

"But you've nothing to worry about, my virtuous friend. This young man," he shook Laerl as he referred to him, "has come of age. He's beyond the time of his

Choosing. It was – interrupted – by my arrival. Who knows? Perhaps he would have become a Woodsward.

"But Laerl will *not* be a Woodsward, of course," he continued. Vok stood Laerl up straight, squared his shoulders and adjusted his torn tunic. "No. He'll be the father of a new race of men. One of the fathers. I get chills whenever I think about it.

"But now that he's of age I think it's only fair to show him all he'll be missing. Or don't you agree?" From an inner pocket in his cloak of faces Vok produced a sprig of white berries.

Thayn interrupted, "Laerl, listen to me. If that's true, wouldn't it only be fair to show Vok all *he's* missing, too? Let me try." Thayn pulled Jad close and kissed him tenderly.

Would Laerl remember tenderness as something suddenly taken away?

Vok couldn't remember it at all.

"What my kiss represents is what you'll be missing, Laerl – respect, honor, affection and love." Thayn embraced Jad.

"This isn't what I want him to see," Vok complained.

Kaden embraced Owan, too, kissing him.

"Enough. Stop it." Vok slapped Laerl until the

Woodswarder complied. "This isn't going well at all.

"Back to our audience, then. Come." They left the preparation room and returned to the stage.

Vok restored the children's hearing and continued. "So, that's what Woodswarder do – except they ruined it." He shoved Laerl back into the audience.

"Now for our next act." Vok continued to set the stage before leaving it. "Ahem. This is the story of a great hero. Of me.

"Here I am." Vok's thought provoked Thayn forward. "My nephew will play my part. Handsome, aren't we? An inquisitive expression, seemingly sincere. Did I mention the family resemblance?"

Thayn bowed against his will. "Applaud," Vok ordered the audience.

The children clapped. Outcasts and men in gray whistled and cheered.

"Thank you," Thayn heard himself say.

Vok brightened. "My nephew, by the way, is visiting me from Eator. Let me tell you about Eator during intermission, children. After tonight's show some of you may join me in planning its destruction. It'll be spectacular.

"And such an unexpected treat. You see, if these fine Woodswarder hadn't attempted to *invade* us –

retaliation against the fair city of my birth – instead of merely ransacking it from afar – would never have occurred to me. Serendipitously, it's perfectly thematic."

Vok watched as Thayn and Kaden exchanged uneasy looks.

"But I digress. Now, our poor hero," Vok continued, "was – misunderstood."

His emotions grew as his pauses lengthened.

"None when he was a child – and none now – " he nodded to Thayn " – none ever – " Vok whispered to himself, shaking his head sadly " – ever realized just how – *special* – he was.

"They've *learned*," he screamed.

He spoke more rapidly. "Let me tell you, children. This young man – his name is Vok – came to your city. After being warmly received by certain women who, alak, are no longer with us, he went straight to see the High Warden." Vok brought Kaden forward and he bowed.

Here Ava refilled her mind. Her thoughts reached out to Thayn and Kaden. They sensed her.

Vok sensed something, too. Before he had time to locate its source, Thayn diverted him, springing upon Kaden with a shout.

Vok returned his attention to the Woodswarder.

"Wait. Oh, well."

Ava refilled Rykos' mind, too.

Vok glanced toward the audience, but only for a moment.

"Oh-h." Kaden's fist found Thayn's jaw. Thayn caught Kaden low on the leg and brought him to the floor. They struggled convincingly against each other. Owan and Jad stood over them, but didn't seem to know what to do.

Vok was delighted.

The time, Thayn realized, was now. Words came to him from the temple of Kala. "*Alak za az kala... Alak za az kala inexeterna...*" He communicated them to the Woodswarder.

Ava and Rykos already knew them by heart.

"*Alak za az kala –* " Thayn recited aloud.

Vok suddenly returned to his senses. He shook off his confusion, realizing his vulnerability. In his travels he himself had discovered the temple of Kala and taken potent incantations for his own, breaking the tablets upon which they were written. Now he heard unex-pected words from those very tablets spoken aloud. "No," he screamed. They comprised an incantation that would recall the stolen spells to the recuperated stone, robbing Vok of his illicit power.

He reached out his hand to Thayn, furious. Light flashed from his fingertips. A bolt struck Thayn and he fell.

"Oh," Ava exclaimed.

"*Alak za az –* " the incantation resounded. This time Kaden spoke its words.

"No," Vok shouted. He adjusted his aim. Another bolt of light brought Kaden to the floor.

Next, without warning, he blasted Jad and Owan. "Just in case." They crumpled.

Vok smiled at the children. A resolute expression froze upon his face.

"*Alak za az –* "

Who was this? He whirled around.

Ava.

Vok found her. "No," he screamed, pointing at her.

Ava was strong. " *– kala... Alak za –* " she continued.

Vok struggled to retain his powers. Another blast from his fingertips and he prevailed.

"Oh." Ava collapsed.

Vok stood motionless for a moment. He waited. Nothing happened.

Rykos wasn't strong. Vok didn't feel his mind.

He knelt next to the youngest one that he could find and whispered, "*Alak za az kala... Alak za az kala inexeterna.*"

Vok didn't hear them among the cries of the others. He adjusted his cloak, eager to get back to his performance. "Well, that was unexpected. As is so often the case, more drama goes on behind the scenes than on the stage.

"And now I've lost my actors. I suppose I'll have to stand in for them all.

"Where were we? Yes. The hero – *I* – came to your city and proceeded to the camp of your High Warden." Vok waited for applause.

"You didn't know, children, that all your lives you have been protected by Woodswarder, did you? Well, in this instance, you *weren't*." Vok paused for laughter.

Kaden lay on the stage floor next to Thayn. Vok continued, "Now, watch how Vok attended to your High Warden. There will be little sport in it at this point, but I don't want to leave out anything that is historically relevant." Vok held out his hand to Kaden and pointed his finger.

"*Alak za az kala...*" Chanting, Rykos stood and walked across the room, leaving the child to whom he had whispered. Vok scrutinized the audience, incredulous. Rykos ducked, but Vok spotted him. The incantation was almost complete. "*Alak za az kala inex –* "

"No," Vok cried, directing a blast at Rykos. Stunned, Rykos staggered backwards. His voice trailed off. Vok smiled triumphantly.

Another voice continued. It was so tiny that Vok couldn't find it, but he heard it. He scanned the children and they scattered, screaming.

" *– in – ex – e – ter – na,*" the tiny voice managed.

The screams of the children were cut short. A final burst of light filled the room.

CHAPTER TWENTY-THREE
Arcane exit

Everyone who remained in the room fell to the floor, stunned by Vok's spell. Jad and Owan were the first to recover. They crawled to Kaden and Thayn.

Kaden revived. He objected to Owan's fussing. "Let me be."

Moments ago Thayn knelt over Jad. Now their roles were reversed. Jad called his name, but Thayn didn't stir.

Owan and Kaden went out among the children. As the children roused they looked with fearful eyes at the Woodswarder – most hadn't seen them prior to the pageant – and at the two newcomers who lay among them. Owan found Rykos and Ava.

"Can you hear me?" he asked them. "Wake up."

Kaden looked around, taking a quick inventory of the Outcasts in the room. Vok was nowhere to be seen.

A child cried, "Where did they go?"

"Who?" Kaden asked.

"My big brother."

"My sisters."

"Where's Laerl?"

Ava sat up and concentrated. "They're in the Center. I can sense them. They're so afraid. He – Vok – has taken them."

Owan exclaimed, "Let's go."

"Can you guide us to them?" Kaden asked, placing a hand on Ava's shoulder.

Her eyes opened wide as she lost her concentration. "Yes."

She led them across the hall and into the Center, all but Thayn and Jad.

Jad called, "Rykos, wait."

Rykos hurried back to him.

"I have to go with them. I'm a Woodsward," Jad explained. "Thayn would expect nothing less of me. Will you stay with him?"

Together they smiled at Thayn. Rykos nodded and knelt at his friend's side. Jad walked a few steps backwards, watching Thayn until he turned and disappeared into the Center.

*

"Can you hear me?" Rykos brushed the hair off his friend's brow.

Thayn was unresponsive.

Rykos talked softly to himself. "What are we up to this time, my friend? Oh, Thayn – why aren't we on our way home from school? But, no, we're here.

"We're in somebody else's school," he continued, looking around. "As if we're living somebody else's life. Why aren't we playing in the fields? Or visiting the marketplace?

"Why don't you hear me?" He patted Thayn on the cheek. He shook him gently. "Come, wake up, Thayn.

"Oh – yes," Rykos interrupted himself. He remembered what Boz had told him. "What a dut I am."

Rykos grew quiet and calm. He waited.

He listened. Yes.

Thayn called out in thought. His plea for help was faint and Rykos strained to hear. He was patient and waited. Thayn's thought grew stronger.

Finally Rykos understood Thayn's request. The incantation. Rykos repeated it for him. "*Alak za az kala –* "

Thayn joined in weakly. "*Alak – za –* "

They completed together, " *– az kala inexeterna.*"

Thayn's expression returned. He sat up and looked around the room. "Where's Vok? Where are the other children?"

*

The others were deep within the Center. Ava hurried along the corridors. The Woodswarder followed her. She pursued a course determined by her sense of the children and her growing familiarity with the Center.

But the Center of Yutor wasn't exactly the same as the Center of Eator and, despite the open doorways, she mistook her way more than once. As they backtracked, Owan grew impatient and grumbled.

"Hush," Kaden reproved him.

*

Thayn stood abruptly. He was wobbly, but stayed upright. "I have to stop them," he exclaimed.

"Ava and Kaden have gone to stop them," Rykos assured Thayn. "You need to rest."

"No. You don't understand. I have to stop Kaden. And Ava." Thayn ran from the room and into the Center.

Rykos stood in confusion. What did Thayn mean? Was he under Vok's spell? Weren't Thayn's thoughts his own?

He was torn between his fear of Thayn's words and concern for the children. The oldest among them – Laerl and those who were deprived of their Choosings by the arrival of Vok – were missing. To those who remained Rykos cautioned, "Stay here and don't wander off. Take care of the little ones."

To the Outcasts he declared, "If any children are harmed, you'll pray for death to relieve you from your suffering." It was a bluff on his part, but he wagered that it would work.

Rykos followed after Thayn. He entered the Center and immediately became lost.

*

Thayn could hear the others ahead, the sound of feet slapping on stone. He remembered their footfall from previous occasions. Beyond them Thayn heard chanting and sobs.

"*Trea abba acca adda…*" Vok chanted words that he had stolen from Jovia.

A second chant challenged his spell. "*Trea baab caac daad…*" Ava's voice rang clear.

"No." Something wasn't right. Thayn ran as fast as he could, fearing that he was already too late. He entered the Hall of Choosing.

It took a moment for him to figure out what was

happening. To one side of the hall were Kaden, Owan and Jad. They pinned Outcasts against the wall.

In front of the Doors of Choosing stood Vok and Ava. Between them, crying, the youth of Yutor cowered, participants in a counterfeit ceremony. Yet again Vok clutched Laerl by the throat.

Prompted by Vok's words, the Third Door cracked open. Ava's words kept it from opening farther.

"*Trea abba acca adda...*"

"*Trea baab caac daad...*"

Vok and Ava struggled with their incantations and against each other. The Third Door inched open only to close again.

"*Trea abba acca adda...*"

"*Trea baab caac daad...*"

Thayn hesitated. It would be better if the situation played out correctly on its own. But would it?

Rykos skidded into the chamber. Thayn called to him, "Stay out of this."

"Thayn, what are you doing?" Rykos asked.

"*Trea abba acca adda...*" Vok weakened.

"*Trea baab caac daad...*" Ava rallied her strength.

"*Trea abba acca adda...* Rykos, you don't understand."

The chanting continued. Did Ava?

The Third Door opened farther and held for a moment. Everyone stared at it in amazement. It moved at Thayn's bidding.

Ava's eyes grew wide. They continued chanting.

"He's here to help Vok," Rykos cried. He turned and looked at the Woodswarder. "Something's happened to him."

"Rykos, don't," Thayn cried. "*Trea abba acca adda*... Ava, it's better to let them go."

"*Trea baab caac daad*... What?"

"The Third Door," Thayn explained quickly, "has one purpose and two positions, closed and open. Provoking both positions at the same time violates a utility of powers greater than Kala himself."

"If this is Kala's teaching," Ava asked, "why don't I already know it? *Trea baab caac daad*..."

"My understanding came as I heard your words spoken together. It's from the tablets."

"Or is it Vok's teaching?"

"No. It's the nature of truth – to make itself known according to need – Jovia explained it to me in the temple of Kala. *Trea abba acca adda*... "

"If *that's* true, then how do – "

"In the greater scheme of things, Ava, to everything there is egress. We must stop chanting before – "

" – before what?"

"Enough of this." Kaden grabbed Jad's Outcast and, still holding his own by the neck, brought their heads together. They fell to the floor. Then he sprang toward Thayn.

"No," Thayn warned him. Kaden tackled Thayn and flung him away from the Doors of Choosing.

"*Trea abba acca adda...*" Vok rallied. The Third Door opened.

"*Trea baab caac daad...*" Kaden joined in the chant. The Third Door shuddered and shrugged. Confounded, it slowly shut.

In response came a faint rumbling. Vok stopped and smiled. "Come," he coaxed the youth of Yutor.

The rumbling grew stronger.

Vok stretched his fingers around Laerl's neck. "Obey me or I'll kill him."

"Oh-h," Laerl cried.

The room trembled underfoot.

"The rest of you stay away or – " Vok threatened and Laerl groaned " – I'll rip out his throat."

With a sharp snap, stone began to split. The room shook. All stared at the wall in amazement, except for Vok and Thayn.

Next to the Third Door, a crack appeared. It grew

up from the floor as high as a man, then cleaved across a short distance and reached down to the floor again.

"The Fourth Door."

It swung open.

The shaking knocked Ava, Rykos and the Woods-warder to the floor.

Using Laerl to gesture, Vok directed those whom he had selected through the Fourth Door. They disappeared, screaming. Gleefully, Vok squealed, "We're off. But, before we go – "

*

" – come, Thayn." Vok's tenor changed. He spoke in the voice that Thayn heard in his head ever since his father's so-called accident. "Come with me.

"We must live together under the trees. There's much I must amend. I'll make up for everything." It was his father's voice.

The others in the Hall of Choosing didn't hear him. Vok spoke to Thayn alone. Despite the shaking that kept the others pinned to the floor, Thayn stood erect.

Now Arlos took shape before him. Generous lips and cool gray eyes. Thayn could hear his heart pounding in his ears. Could everyone hear it?

"Thayn, you're strong and brave. You're deserving. You're everything I've ever wanted, and I'm here to reward you – in *perpetuity*."

As his father's son, Thayn was no match for Vok's persuasions. How simple it would be to follow his father and Arlos through the Fourth Door.

Another voice called to him. "Thayn?"

It seemed so far away. "Jad?"

Thayn turned. Jad struggled to his feet. The shaking intensified. Jad stood to one side of Thayn and, beside the open Fourth Door, Arlos stood to the other. Thayn looked from one familiar face to the other. Both of them offered him alternatives, both immediate and everlasting. It was an unanticipated contest.

Whom would Thayn choose?

With Jad, Thayn felt complete. Jad gladly and easily offered Thayn everything that he ever wanted. The promise of Arlos' attention, however, made Thayn feel that, without it, he would be forever empty inside – and here Arlos stood soliciting him. How simply he could lose himself – and find himself – in Arlos' company.

Thayn again sensed that something wasn't right – this was too good to be true. The realization returned him to the moment. "No," he managed. His mother's sense of rightness prevailed.

"Don't let him deceive you," Jad warned.

"Ignore him." Jad's intrusion interrupted Vok's

concentration. Arlos' face reverted to Zayn for a moment until, contorting, it reappeared as its owner, uglier than ever.

Thayn resisted his uncle. His knees gave way and he sank to the floor.

Vok regarded his nephew with a snort. "Fool." Whispering quick words, he slipped through the Fourth Door.

*

Vok disappeared. With a violent crack, the Fourth Door disappeared, too. The shaking stopped. Everyone in the Hall of Choosing looked around in astonishment. The room seemed suddenly empty.

Vok and the stolen youth of Yutor were gone. Outcasts lay unconscious on the floor. Ava, Rykos and the Woodswarder turned to Thayn. "What have we done?"

CHAPTER TWENTY-FOUR
Perpetuity

Kaden ran to the wall where the Fourth Door had closed and pounded on it. He recoiled in pain. The stone was hot.

"Where have they gone?" Ava asked.

Thayn shook his head. He didn't feel like sharing his suspicions at the moment.

"Maybe you should try those spells again," Owan suggested. "Would it help if I pretended to be Vok?"

"No," Kaden objected.

Words of wisdom came to Thayn from a surprising source. "There is plenty we *do* know and plenty for us to *do* without resorting to pointless conjecture."

Ava explained to the others, "My father always said that. Thayn's referring, I think, to the children we left with – " she looked from Jad to Rykos " – oh, no. Who's taking care of the children?"

They ran to the lecture hall adjoining the school. The children were unattended, but safe.

*

The men in gray collapsed at Vok's passing. They had been forced to do reprehensible things and, without Vok, their minds unraveled and they died. Except for Kaden and the children, none of Yutor survived.

Released from Vok's spell, Outcasts returned to themselves. Those guarding the children were cowards and already had slunk away fearing Rykos' threat.

*

Thayn and Ava decided that their priority was to free Yutor of the remaining Outcasts. Rykos and the Woodswarder would clear the Center of them while Ava restored the doorways.

Kaden led the way. His blue eyes darted and his nostrils flared. Unwanted guests took refuge in the High Chamber and Hall of Choosing. They scattered through different doors. The Woodswarder separated and followed them.

Rykos joined Owan and they made chase together. Owan turned down a side hallway leaving Rykos on his own. Almost immediately Outcasts were chasing Rykos back the way that he came.

Meanwhile Ava touched the walls and whispered.

A door behind Rykos closed and the Outcasts slammed against it. They fled in the opposite direction.

The Center was purged. Door by door, its safety was resealed. Cracked stone sighed and healed as the campaign continued outside its walls.

Rykos decided that he might be more helpful if he joined Ava. They attended to the children while the Woodswarder labored to rid the city of Vok's former army.

New powers of Kala came to Thayn in response to need. He shared them freely with Kaden, Owan and Jad. They appeared terrible before the Outcasts. Yutor was emptied of its vermin. The rats fled, too.

Ava sat and analyzed the children. They brimmed with fear and horror. She did her best to ease their thoughts, but most of them were beyond repair. Ava was forced to close their minds. Their pained expressions softened and they no longer cried.

*

Rykos found them suitable quarters within a cluster of dwellings under tall trees in the fields. It offered surroundings familiar to them all. After the Woodswarder returned they took the children there.

Thayn and Jad hunted for mushrooms. Kaden and Owan picked redfruit and Rykos found grain that had been ignored by the Outcasts and rats. He and Ava baked bread and they all enjoyed a welcome meal.

"I've found places for us all to sleep," Rykos told the others. Already some of the children, relieved of their thoughts, slipped into untroubled slumber.

Kaden announced, "I'll share in the supervision of the children, but I won't sleep here." He glanced uneasily at Thayn. "Owan will come for me at the appropriate time."

He left.

"He mistrusts me," Thayn acknowledged.

"Not you," Owan explained. "Vok."

"But – "

"Go with him, Owan," Ava suggested. "We'll be fine.

"Children, come with me," she told those who were awake. They followed her inside. Rykos carried those who were already asleep.

Thayn and Jad slept under the trees. The branches overhead were inviting, but they wanted to be at hand in case Ava or Rykos needed them.

*

The next morning Kaden, Owan and Jad stayed with the children. Ava and Rykos joined Thayn at the temple. He gave them each a berry the colors of which hadn't been seen since the Ancient Days. The city of Yutor was broken and burnt. Representing the Genexus, Ministration and Woodswarder, channeling primordial energy, they began restoration of the city.

They walked to the Ring and held their palms to the ground. Saplings sprang into maturity before them, reaching high to repair the great vaulted canopy. The Wooden Wall rebuilt itself. They returned through the Fallow Field. Herbs underfoot grew tender and untrampled. Finally, they combined their thoughts and turned to the city. They all reached a palm to it. Broken stone recollected itself and rose up out of the rubble.

Thayn, Ava and Rykos returned to their dwelling in the fields. The beleaguered city was cleansed and reclaimed. Aside from themselves, however, and the stricken children, Yutor was empty. No berry grew that would remedy that aspect of Yutor's plight.

*

Ava, Rykos and the Woodswarder attended to the children in rotations. It was Thayn, Jad and Owan's turn. The others walked through the city, visiting the empty marketplace, classrooms and gardens. They sat on the temple steps and looked out at the Fallow Field. They shared their thoughts about Yutor's future. No matter what plan they considered, it would require determination and sacrifice.

They prayed to Kala. Their collective will grew strong as a mission was conceived. From Eator they would ask permission to recruit Genexus, Ministration and Woodswarder to resettle Yutor. "It's difficult to think about the city without the two of you," Kaden told Ava and Rykos.

*

The following morning Thayn overslept. An earlier dream revisited him. Kaden's arm met Jad's and it broke. *Crack.* Jad's arm met Owan's and it broke. *Crack.* Owan's met an arm that Thayn didn't recognize, and then another, and another. Their cries came to him as the thoughts of Yodin.

"Yodin, what are you doing in my dream?" Thayn roused with a start, sitting up. Yodin wasn't there.

It was already morning. The others, awake, were staring at him. "Are you all right?" Jad asked.

"I'm not sure." Thayn shook his head. "Ava, will you join me in the Chamber of Ages?"

*

Returning from a brief consultation in the Chamber of Ages, Thayn requested, "Owan. Jad. Will you accompany me on a journey?

"A journey?" Kaden asked.

"I need to speak with Yodin."

*

Kaden remained in Yutor with Ava and Rykos. By default they became, respectively, High Warden, High Minister and sole Senior Peer of Yutor. They spoke together of the city's future, its design and the contributions that they hoped to offer it. Rykos easily realized that Kaden and Ava were in Yutor to stay. What, he wondered, would Aryla say when he asked her to join them?

*

Thayn, Owan and Jad traveled to Tordawn. Outcasts fled before them. The Woodswarder rode rafts down the river and the Blue One met them in the lake. He and several companions transported their guests to the far shore.

Yodin waited for them. They continued to an outpost near the clearing of the Green Folk. After Thayn met in private with Yodin, the Woodswarder climbed into the tallest trees.

"Owan, you have sharp eyes," Thayn said. "Look out into the desert."

Jad and Thayn saw sand that spread forever away from Kala, uninterrupted. Owan, however, squinted at something where the desert met the sky. "Oh," he exclaimed. "Another body of land? And – "

"What do you see?" Jad asked.

"A cliff – and in its face – "

"Yes?"

"It's the face of Vok." Both he and Jad looked at Thayn, who nodded.

"Yodin sensed him and came to me in a dream."

Jad asked, "Vok?"

"Why?" Owan asked.

"To establish a new land – one to rival Kala."

"A land of Vok?"

"How is this possible?"

"In the same way there is a land of Kala – it's difficult to explain," Thayn replied, " – but yes, a land of Vok."

"Horrible."

"Ava confirmed by the throwing their stones that those Vok took with him are of age. Only – "

"What?" Owan squinted again at the horizon.

Thayn tilted his head.

Jad asked, "What do you hear, Thayn?"

"The throwing of the stones – it doesn't make you brave. I hear – crying. The crying of children."